WINDRUSH
CHILD

For my twin sister Velda, because I really want her to
read a book, and she should start with this one.

Published in the UK by Scholastic Children's Books, 2020
Euston House, 24 Eversholt Street, London, NW1 1DB

A division of Scholastic Limited
London ~ New York ~ Toronto ~ Sydney - Auckland
Mexico City ~ New Delhi ~ Hong Kong

ISBN 978 07023 0272 5

A CIP catalogue record for this book is available from the British Library.

Printed by CPI Group (UK) Ltd, Croydon CR0 4YY

Papers used by Scholastic Children's Books are made from wood grown in
sustainable forests.

3 5 7 9 10 8 6 4

www.scholastic.co.uk

WINDRUSH CHILD

BENJAMIN ZEPHANIAH

Series Consultant:

Tony Bradman

■SCHOLASTIC

Author's Note

Warning. This story contains strong language that some readers might find offensive. In reality, when you are on the receiving end of some of these words you are very offended, but I think I would be cheating readers if I were to gloss over some of the language that is used by racists. As a young boy in school, I remember people saying, 'Sticks and stone may break my bones, but names can never hurt me,' and I didn't believe them. Names hurt me. I was called names because of the colour of my skin, because I was dyslectic, even because of the way I spoke, and those words really hurt. Fortunately, I used words to fight back, and I became a writer.

Now I use my words to give voice to people like Leonard, the main character of this book. He's just doing what people have been doing for thousands of years, moving around the planet. When people move they always have to deal with the trauma of leaving the country of their birth, and then the struggle to fit into their new home. I've heard adults talking about this for years, but I wanted to explore what it was like for their children. So, mind your language, and please understand that the language contained in this book is here because the author, a Windrush child, is keeping it real.

Prologue

I didn't just appear here. I've been on a journey. I've lived a life. I wasn't blown in by the wind. I didn't land here by chance. My roots are deep. They run deep in the memories of my ancestors. As deep as the foundations of the first civilizations built on this earth. As deep as the deepest roots of the oldest African tree down in this earth. Deep. Deeper than the human imagination will allow. Deep, I'm telling you. So I shouldn't be judged by where I am now. Yes, I'm desperate; yes, I'm in need, but I'm no beggar. I sit in this horrendous place alone and in need of others, but I am a family man. I'm told that men have died in places like this. I am told that men have died in this very place, but I have no intention of dying here. I have lived too long, and come too far, to die in the hands of those who do not love me. I have worked too hard, and struggled too much to die on this cold, concrete bench, alone. They call me old, but

I must live.

I have cried, but trust me, that is not a sign of weakness. Crying made me strong. Crying made me human. Crying reminded me that the biggest man you ever did see was once just a baby, and he cried too. I'm a man, and I cried. It's the injustice that hurts. As I sit in the windowless room, with its cold magnolia walls that are covered in distressed graffiti, and the last messages of hopeless, miserable men, I seek love and strength. Because I know my place, and it's not here.

Chapter One

I love history. I am history. We made history. We were the people of Maroon Town, Jamaica. This is where I was born on 15 October 1947. But long before I was born – I'm talking hundreds and hundreds of years ago – the Taíno and Arawak lived in Jamaica. They were farmers who used to create fertilizers to help grow cassava, peanuts, corn and beans. They used to trade pottery, woodcarvings and crops with other Amazonian tribes, and although it wasn't perfect – they lived in peace for hundreds of years. I didn't learn any of this at school in Jamaica. In school I just got taught English history. It was my grandma, my mum and the elders in Maroon Town who told me about the real history of Jamaica. It wasn't written down, but passed on by word of mouth, from one generation to the next. They even taught me songs and poems about our history, but we weren't allowed to sing those songs in school. Instead we had to sing 'God Save the Queen' and 'Rule Britannia'.

In the hills outside Maroon Town lived my favourite family friend, Brother Book. He had very dark skin and long golden dreadlocks. He lived a natural life, up high in a hut with no electricity and no running water. He didn't even have any books, but he was called Brother Book because he had so much knowledge. He would come to our house for food sometimes. One afternoon, as I sat with Grandma eating cashew nuts, he asked me a question.

"So, young Leonard. Tell me, who discovered Jamaica?"

I thought the answer was easy. "Christopher Columbus," I said enthusiastically.

But as I looked at my grandma, she raised an eyebrow, so I knew something was wrong.

Brother Book smiled and stroked his long beard as he spoke to me with his deep voice.

'So what about de Taíno an' de Arawak people? Christopher Columbus only came here in 1494. People have lived on this island for thousands of years before dat. So how comes you don't think one of them discovered it?'

'That's what it sey at school,' I replied. 'That's what it sey in all of de books.'

'Yes. But who wrote the books?' he said. 'Europeans

2

wrote history from their point of view. We must remember that when Christopher Columbus landed his ship here, flying a Spanish flag with a Spanish crew, everything changed. The Taíno, the Arawak, and all the other people who were here were killed by the Spanish. Those that weren't killed by them died from the diseases they brought with them.'

Then Grandma joined in.

'Then de Spanish began to bring Africans here by force, and mek dem work as slaves. Many slaves would run away an' live in de mountains an' some of dem would try to fight de Spanish. Dem fight very hard you know, but they were outnumbered.'

Brother Book interrupted gently.

'Other European countries were trying to tek control of land in Africa an' de Americas to expand their slave trade, but de Spanish held on to Jamaica.'

We all chewed on our cashew for a moment when a question came to me.

'So why don't we speak Spanish?'

'Because,' replied Brother Book with eyes wide open, 'in 1665, de English fought de Spanish for Jamaica an' won. More an' more Africans were then brought to de island to work in de sugar plantations. De English were getting tea from India, an' so they needed sugar for their tea an' cakes.'

I was surprised. 'All dat for tea and cakes?' I asked.

'Yes,' said Grandma. 'Later they started to deal in cotton an' all kind of minerals, but it started because Europeans had sweet teeth. Now you know Manchester in England?' she asked, looking at me.

'Yes, Grandma,' I replied.

'Well not far from Manchester there's a port called Liverpool. Ships sailed from there an' other ports like Bristol an' London, an' they travelled to Africa. In Africa they captured people, and sometimes they got corrupt Africans to capture people for them an' they took those captured Africans to Jamaica or other Caribbean islands to work as slaves.'

'We are descended from those Africans,' said Brother Book.

'That's right,' Grandma continued. 'Then, before they returned home they filled de ships with sugar, fruits an' other goods for de people in England to enjoy.'

'This,' Brother Book said, 'was called the transatlantic slave trade. A triangular trade route across the ocean from Africa, to the Caribbean then on to Britain. This evil slave triangle made de slave traders a lot of money for many years.'

Brother Book and Grandma went on to tell me that the slave trade continued until the nineteenth century, and that it wasn't just the English and the Spanish who were doing it. The Dutch, the French, Danish and even the Swedes were making money by enslaving human beings.

'But,' said Brother Book, waving his finger in the air as in the direction of England. 'It was de English who boasted that they were de biggest and the best, followed closely by de Portuguese.'

I used to love sitting on the veranda talking with Grandma, and it was even more special when Brother Book was there. The more I learned about slavery, the more terrible it seemed, but I wanted to learn as much as I could.

In Maroon Town I could see that most of the people were of African descent but there were also people from China, India and Syria. I used to wonder where they came from until Brother Book explained to me that when slavery was over the British brought lots of Chinese and the Indians to Jamaica to work. They were paid very little, some were not paid at all, and most people thought it was not much better than slavery. The Lebanese and the Syrians came as refugees, and there were other Europeans who came simply because they wanted to live in a warm, beautiful country.

Chapter Two

My mum worked as a domestic, cleaning people's houses. She worked hard and spent a lot of time at work. Sometimes she worked seven days a week. She just never said no if someone wanted their house cleaned because we needed the money. I spent most of my time with my grandma, which was great because she let me do more or less anything. When I was eight years old my mum bought me a red kite in the shape of a bird. One really hot day when she was at work, I was playing with it so much that my neck started to hurt, and I got really dizzy. Grandma told me to sit on the veranda floor, then she sat on her chair behind me and rubbed castor oil into my neck.

After a few minutes of rubbing she asked, 'How it feel now?'

'Good,' I said.

'When your granddad was alive, me used to rub him neck all de time with this oil. He was a good man, he was.'

Although I never knew my granddad I found out a lot about him from Grandma. She had a couple of grainy black and white photos at the side of her bed, but sometimes she would take them and hold them in her hand as she sat in her chair on the veranda.

'Your granddad was born on the twentieth of July, 1906, and I was born on the twentieth August de same year. That is amazing, eh? And we born just down de road from each other.'

She stopped massaging me when a blue hummingbird with flashes of red and yellow on its feathers caught our attention. Its wings flapped faster than the eye could see, yet it hovered perfectly in the same place as it drank sap from the ceiba tree next to the house.

Grandma smiled. 'You see how nature smart. Nature created a bird that can move so fast, without moving. That is wonderful.'

'Yes,' I replied. 'My kite can't do that.'

'Your kite is man-made. Man does one thing, nature does another. You should not envy nature; you must live with nature. Your kite and the hummingbird can share de sky, as long as you behave and don't start believing you own de sky.'

She continued massaging me and speaking.

'Singers keep singing saying we should be free

like de bird in the tree. De bird is free to fly, an' we should be free to walk. During de days of slavery, we, de Maroons, fought against de slave traders, an' de greatest freedom fighter Jamaica had was called Nanny of de Maroons. She led our people in many battles against de British. She was never a slave an' she said that no one deserved to be a slave. She inspired us to fight against slavery, an' even when slavery was over, we kept fighting against all de foreigners who tried to control Jamaica. That's not because we want to be like the hummingbird; this was because we believed in our right to be free. We, the Maroons, should always remember Nanny. Nanny taught us never to give up our freedom.'

As Grandma finished speaking, the hummingbird flew away, a bolt of lightning cracked in the sky, then the thunder roared, and the rain came. I jumped up off the ground and we went into Grandma's room. In the room I sat next to her dressing table where she kept her photos of Granddad. Grandma noticed me looking at the photos. One was of Granddad and Grandma together, and the other was one of him on his own. They were both taken around the same time. It was strange to think of the man in the photos as my granddad, he looked so young.

'Him was only nineteen then,' Grandma said. 'Just

one year before your dad was born. See how him look nice in him suit?'

'Yes, him look fine,' I replied.

'He was a true Maroon,' she said. 'When your dad was thirteen years old your granddad used to take him into de mountains an' teach him how to live off de land. Him teach him how to survive by finding food in de wild, an' how to find his way through the bush. Most importantly, your granddad taught him to value freedom.'

She reached over to me, pointing to the photos, so I took them and handed them to her. The rain was falling heavily outside as she looked at the photos for a long minute.

'No to the British, no to the Spanish, yes to freedom he used to sey, but then he had to mek a big decision. World War Two was on an' de British needed help. They were asking for men and women from Jamaica to help them fight the war. Granddad wasn't sure what to do.'

This was a part of my family history that I could not understand.

'Why him leave Jamaica, Grandma?'

'At the time many Jamaicans thought that no one from de Caribbean should help Britain. They said World War Two was a white man's war. Jamaica was still run by de British, so other people believed that if Jamaicans fought with de British, when de war was over, it would help Jamaicans get independence. Your granddad said Adolf Hitler was de enemy who hated all of us. He thought Hitler was de worse man in the world, so he decided he had to join the British Army to get rid of him. When the fighting was done his plan was to come back to Jamaica and campaign for independence from the British. In 1939, he passed his medical test. He went to England for military training, and then he was sent to fight de bad people who invaded France. But then in May of 1940 he was killed in what dem call de battle of Arras.'

She paused for a while and stared at the photos in her hand. I could see tears running down her cheeks. She looked directly at me with her red watery eyes and said, 'You know, Leonard, all I got from de British government was a letter saying that he died in action an' was buried where he fell. He wasn't even listed as dead back in Britain.'

I had never seen my grandma cry and I didn't know what to do.

'Can I get something for you, Grandma?' I said, not knowing what to say. 'Drink, Grandma. You want a drink?'

'No. It's all right,' she said, smiling through her tears.

'When me lose your granddad, I was heartbroken. I was feeling so bad that I didn't want to live, but your dad, who was only fourteen years old at the time, gave me the strength to continue And now, you, you handsome chap, you give me strength to continue.'

My grandma continued to raise my dad on her own, but she said he was really raised by the whole village. Neighbours began to take him to the bush to teach him how to survive, and she always had people around her to help when she needed money. My dad started to sell vegetables to earn money for Grandma when he was still going to school. When he met my mum, Rita, he didn't have enough money to build a house of his own, so they stayed at my grandma's house. She wanted the company anyway. Then I was born.

Grandma was always talking to me, but Mum never talked much about her life. She just told me she didn't have any contact with her family, and she had a life of suffering. A life of trials and tribulations. She told me that meeting my dad brought her great happiness, and my birth brought her more happiness. She told me that dad was also happy of course, but he was only happy for a while. Then it was as if there was a cloud hanging over him. He felt that he could not continue to feed his family by selling vegetables and doing odd jobs. He felt that the family were poor because of him.

The British government had posters all over Jamaica telling people that they would be welcome to come to Britain, to help rebuild the country because the war had left it in ruins. Jamaicans were told on radio and in town halls that Britain was the 'land of opportunity' where 'the streets would soon be paved with gold'. They were told that they would be greeted with the great British hand of friendship, because they were British citizens, and they were welcomed in the mum country. My dad couldn't resist. He felt that he had to do something, for Britain and for himself, so seven months after I was born, he boarded a ship and sailed to England. He promised Mum that after a few years of work he would return, and everything would be all right.

So my dad left when I was just a baby. As soon as he landed he sent a letter back to Mum and Grandma, and a postcard for me. The postcard had a picture of the ship that took him to England. It was called the *Empire Windrush*. On the back of the card he wrote,

I am a Windrush man,
so you, my child,
are a Windrush Child.

Chapter Three

Although my dad wasn't there, my earliest memories of growing up in Jamaica were fun and carefree. I felt safe and loved. The weather was always fine in Maroon Town and it was safe. The roads were not good enough for cars to drive fast, so the most dangerous things on the roads were the cows. Sometimes they would block the roads in small groups, or, if they got angry, they would run after people. They ran after me a few times but I would never let them catch up with me. Like most black people in Jamaica we didn't have a lot of money, but I never felt poor. In fact, I never saw how rich people lived until Mum got a job cleaning a big house up in the hills. She took me up there one day before I went to school, and I was shocked at what I saw. When Mum opened the gate the big red brick house was still far away, then as we walked towards it two big dogs ran in our direction, barking angrily, but Mum called their names and they calmed down. As we reached the house a Jamaican man came out. He was very thin and old, and when he smiled I could only see four teeth in his mouth.

'This is Walter,' said Mum. 'Him is de caretaker. Him look after all de land, an' do all de handiwork. This is my son, Leonard,' she said to Walter with pride.

Walter reached out to shake my hand. I had never shaken anyone's hand before, but I knew what to do. I reached out too and we shook hands.

'How are you, young Leonard?' he asked.

'I'm fine, sir,' I replied. 'Do you live in this big house, sir?' I asked, looking beyond him to the house.

'No,' he replied as he smiled. 'I live in a small little hut at de back. I just fix anything that need fixing.'

'Is English people live here,' said Mum. 'Dem doing business in Kingston, so dem away for a few days.'

Walter went to work trimming trees with the dogs following him, and Mum took me into the house and quickly showed me around. The floors were all covered with white marble tiles, the furniture was dark brown oak, and the walls were covered with paintings of old white people with curly white wigs. At the back of the house was a large swimming pool, and beyond the swimming pool there were trees. I could see part of a building through the trees, and Mum told me that this was where Walter lived.

'This is how rich people live,' she said. 'The couple who own this house have house in England, house in Australia, an' house in Jamaica. I come here once a week an' Walter is here all de time, and I only see the couple a few times a year. Them always on de move. Them have money.' She looked at a clock on the wall and shouted, 'School.'

We left the house and she rushed me down the garden to the gate, and from there I ran to school.

I had heard some people talking about how rich white people lived, but even after seeing it I wasn't impressed. I couldn't understand why two people could live in such a big house, and then not spend much time there. Then I thought maybe this is how all people lived in England. Could they all have friends who were kings and queens? Did they all travel all over the world? Did they all live in big houses with lots of land?

In England my dad found a job as a bus driver. He was always writing and telling us what he was doing and that made me want to see him even more. I used to think about how good it would be if he was a driver in Jamaica. I couldn't imagine him driving people around who were friends of kings and queens and lived in big houses, but he was earning enough money to send some for us every few months. We loved getting and sending

15

letters to Dad, but back then it really took time. If we wanted to write, we had to use special blue airmail paper. The paper would have to be folded into its own envelope, and then someone, (usually me), would walk into town to post it. It would then be put with letters from other parts of the island and taken to the airport. A plane would leave for England just once a week, and when it arrived in England the post would be sorted in London. From London it would be sent to Manchester, and then posted through Dad's letterbox. If we were lucky it would take two weeks. Dad had to do the reverse if he wrote to us, but he told us he lived near a Post Office.

We weren't rich. I didn't think we needed much, because I was never hungry, and I felt as if I lived in a very special place. The only thing I really lacked was my dad. Everyone took care of me, but I still missed and wanted my dad, and I missed him most of all when I saw other children playing with their dads. It wasn't jealousy. I just felt like something was missing from my life, but I kept reminding myself that Mum said he would be coming back soon. I wasn't sure what soon meant, but I was really looking forward to that day.

At our house in Maroon Town we could always hear the sounds of birds chirping as if talking to each other, and the sounds of crickets, frogs and croaking lizards. Even in the middle of the night it was never completely silent. We had a mango tree, a grapefruit tree, an orange tree, a coconut tree and many banana trees. Every day, I would try a different fruit to see when they were ripe and ready for everyone else to eat. That was my excuse. Sometimes, if I ate something too soon I would get stomachache and I would be told to stay away from that fruit until it fell from the tree. But for some strange reason, I always went back, and I would keep getting bellyache. We also grew cashew nuts, yams, sweet potatoes, pumpkins and lots of other vegetables. People would travel from all over Maroon Town to taste our food. When ripe, everything was so healthy and delicious.

I didn't need a big house. Playing on the grounds around our small house and running around in the bush meant that my clothes were always dirty, but the clothes I wore to school were always spotless. The girls wore a green pinafore with a white blouse, and the boys wore a brown shirt with brown short trousers. In classes we had to pay attention to the teacher; we could only speak when spoken to; we walked from one place to another in silence and we had to be polite at all times. When we spoke to the teachers, we had to call them Madam or Sir.

Although there were many white people living in Jamaica, we didn't see them often, but in every classroom in school there was a picture of the Queen. We were taught about many of the queens and kings of England and Britain, we even had to sing English nursery rhymes, but when I went home my mum and my grandma would teach me Jamaican history, and Jamaican nursery rhymes.

The roads were originally made for donkeys and horses, not for cars, so they were very rough, and when the rains were heavy, the roads would flood and break up. People would come and fix them, but they would only last until the next heavy rain came, and then they'd need fixing again. The good thing was it never got cold in Jamaica. It got cool, but never cold. The sun shone almost every day, but our biggest fear was hurricanes. Between June and November every year the hurricanes would come. Sometimes we could feel them out in the sea, sometimes they would hit other islands in the Caribbean, and sometimes they would hit Jamaica. Trees would get blown over, houses would get blown away, crops would get ruined, and animals and humans would get killed. I loved life with my family in Maroon Town, but I feared the hurricanes.

Chapter Four

Late one afternoon in March 1958, I was kicking a ball around in front of the house. The evening was cool and I could smell Grandma's cooking floating out from the kitchen. I was tired. I had spent most of the day playing football with some friends in the town, and I couldn't wait for Grandma to finish making dinner. When the food was ready, she called me. I kicked the ball away and ran inside.

My grandma would cook often and everything she touched was delicious. She could add her herbs and spices to anything and make it work, but today it was black-eyed peas stew, with rice and callaloo. My grandma always prayed before we ate but, today, there was a sadness in her voice. I had never seen her sweat before. Even when it was hot, she somehow always managed to stay cool. I hoped she wasn't becoming ill. My eyes darted between her and my mum. Something was just not right. She began to share out the food silently for a while with my mum sitting there looking like she had done something wrong. Then Grandma spoke to me.

'I'm really missing your granddad,' she said. 'Today is our wedding anniversary. He used to love this meal. His eyes would be gleaming, but he would never wait for me to put it on the plate, you know. He'd whip it out of my hand like he'd never seen food before. He was a good man, he was.'

When Grandma was talking about Granddad she would often end what she was saying with, 'he was a good man, he was.' I could see pain on her face, and I felt her pain.

'Yes, Grandma. Him was a very good man. Everybody tell me how good him was,' I said.

Despite never knowing Granddad personally, sometimes Grandma touched my heart when she spoke about him, because most of the time she didn't talk about him as if he was dead; she spoke as if they were in a long-distance relationship. She used to talk about the next time she would see him, as if she really had plans to see him again, or like she knew they were going to meet again.

I never liked seeing Grandma sad so I changed the subject and told her about the boys I had been playing with. One of them was called Karl Massey, and he went to the big school. In just over a year, I would be going to the same school, so I was telling them how good it would be to have a friend there. Grandma said, 'That's nice,' but didn't seem that interested. I began to tell them about how I was nervous, but looking forward to going to big school, and how I would try my best to study hard, but then my mum stopped eating. She placed her fork down on the table and looked at me. I thought I had done something really wrong and racked my brain to figure out what it was.

'Now, Leonard,' said Mum. 'Your father has been working very hard driving buses in a England.'

'I know,' I replied, wondering what this could all be about.

Grandma was eating her food as if she knew what was coming, but I wasn't sure. Mum's face showed no emotion. She just played with her fork in the food as she spoke.

'You know he went there so we could have a better life here?'

'I know,' I said. I felt some tension in the room. I felt some good news coming. My heart raced.

'Well, I have something to tell you,' Mum said.

'Yes!' I shouted, throwing my hands in the air. 'Yes. At last he's coming home. Dad's coming home.'

'No,' said Mum.

'What?' I shouted as my arms flopped down at my sides.

'No,' she said calmly. 'We are going to join him.'

'No!' I said forcefully as I could. 'That's not what you said was going to happen. You told me he was coming here. This is our home. You said he was soon coming back where he belonged.'

'Him change him mind,' Mum said.

I started feeling angry.

'He can't just change him mind,' I yelled.

'Leonard, don't raise your voice at the table, you hear?' Grandma interrupted, 'and listen to your mum.'

I looked into my mum's eyes, and she looked into mine.

'He sent some money for your grandma,' she said. 'And he will keep sending money to her, but him want something different for us. Me and your grandma agree. He has saved up enough money for us to join him in England.'

I bowed my head. I didn't want to look at them. 'Don't worry,' said Grandma. 'Everything will be all right.'

I began to think of all the things I would miss in Jamaica, the bush, the fruit, school, and Grandma. I took some deep breaths to stop myself from crying.

22

'It no so bad,' said Grandma.

With my head still bowed I just about managed to say to Mum, 'You promised me that Dad was coming back to me. You said, this is our home, and one day soon he will come home. You told me lies.'

'Don't call your mum a liar,' said Grandma.

'Leonard, we are going to England to be with your dad an' start a new life,' Mum said. 'That's de way it's going to be, an' there's nothing you can do 'bout it.'

For the first time in my life I really wanted to shout at my mum. I wanted to walk out. I wanted to leave the house and be alone. But I was taught never to be disrespectful to my elders. Grandma was looking at me, Mum was looking at me, and it struck me. There really was nothing I could do about it.

Chapter Five

We spent a couple of weeks preparing to leave. I was
miserable, but I couldn't show it. As a ten-year-old I
couldn't argue with my elders – it just wasn't done. If
I tried to simply talk about it, the conversation always
ended up with Mum or Grandma telling me that the
decision had been made, and that there was nothing I
could do about it. Once when I asked Mum what she
felt about leaving she sounded full of happiness and said,
'England will change our lives for ever. We are so lucky
to have the chance to go to such a wonderful place.'

Then another time when I asked her, she seemed
sad. She sighed and said, 'Well, it's a long way to go,
and we're leaving everything that we know behind, but
we are doing this for you.' I didn't see it that way. I was
happy with my coconut tree, my mango tree, and all
other things I loved. I didn't think I needed anything
else, apart from my dad maybe, but I wanted my dad
in Jamaica.

I didn't know much about England. At school I learned about some of their kings and queens, and about the big British Empire, but I didn't know what it was really like. Karl Massey told me it was very cold. He said sometimes birds would drop out of the sky because they froze as they were flying. But my teacher said it gets really hot in England. She read me a poem about daffodils and said daffodils grow where it's hot. I was so confused at their different answers, I ended up asking Brother Book. 'England is a place of four seasons,' he told me. 'It is more complicated than just hot and cold.'

People kept telling me that life would be good in England, and deep down I wanted it to be. I tried to get excited about the change of country. I tried to imagine myself in a country that sounded modern, where the people were richer, but I couldn't. My heart would sink when I thought about how I would miss my friends, my school, Grandma and Maroon Town. Sometimes I cried, but I always cried when I was alone, and the night before we left I slept very little because I cried so much.

The next day I stood looking at our suitcases, dressed in a suit my mum bought for the journey, a suit that was too big for me. The suit felt heavy and hot – too hot for the Jamaican heat. I took the postcard that my dad had sent to me and I put it in my inside pocket. Then I went to my grandma and held her hand as tightly as I could. I had a feeling that I would never see her again. She looked directly into my eyes and said three words that I have never forgotten.

'Lions always roar.' Her voice was fierce.

'What does that mean?' I asked.

'Never be afraid to speak your mind. When the lion roars it's only telling you how it feels.'

The sun had blessed Grandma's skin so beautifully that she shone, and the way her voice had aged gave it power.

'When you arrive in England,' she said. 'There might be some people there that don't like you, but Leonard, let me tell you something: hatred is always a reflection of the hater. You are a lion. Speak truth always and do good, so that good will follow you.'

I had spent so much of my life with my grandma I felt like my heart was being pulled from my chest as we said goodbye. She was very matter of fact.

'What must be done, must be done,' she said. It wasn't that easy for me. I was losing my friends in Maroon Town, the fruit trees and my vegetables, and most importantly, my grandma. I just couldn't understand how any of that was going to make life better for me. If they wanted me to be happy, why didn't my dad just come home?

Mum woke me up very early in the morning. I

was so tired she had to shake me to get me to open my eyes, and as soon as I did I could smell the plantains that Grandma was cooking. We had packed the suitcase the night before, but Mum was in a hurry. She only slowed down when we sat down to eat breakfast. It was only then that we heard the roosters crowing in the distance. I had never been up before them. Throughout breakfast Grandma was giving Mum messages for Dad. It was still dark when we started eating, but by the time we had finished it was light. After breakfast, as the day started to warm, Grandma bent down and hugged me on the veranda.

'You must be a good boy over there, you hear?'

'Yes, Grandma,' I replied.

'An' you must study hard so we can proud of you. All right?'

'Yes, Grandma,' I said.

I wanted to tell her how much I didn't want to go, but I knew I had lost that argument. I was still holding Grandma's hand as she hugged Mum, but then the time had come. I reluctantly released Grandma's hand and walked to the road to get the bus to the centre of town.

From the centre of Maroon Town we took an old bus to Kingston, the capital city of Jamaica. I had only been to Kingston once before. I was two years old, and I don't remember it, but I was told that I hated riding the bus. My mum said that I had screamed for the entire journey, and I wasn't surprised if it was anything like this bus. It was packed with people with their arms and legs hanging out of the windows. Some sat on the roof, and there was even a goat being sheltered under a man's coat. The driver was more interested in the banana he was eating than the bend we were approaching, so when he took the bend people had to hang on for their lives. A lady's suitcase fell from the roof of the bus, but the driver didn't even stop to get it! Instead he accelerated, jolting us forward, then backwards, and then forward again.

'Can you stop driving like a madman, please?' my mum shouted. 'There are children on the bus, you know!'

The driver grunted something under his breath and just threw the skin of his banana out of the window. If my mum expected an answer, she was not going to get it from him. I was really hoping that my dad wasn't a bus driver like this bus driver.

We spent the day in Kingston; the streets were swarming with people and roads were full of cars. Here, the buildings were bigger, the cars were faster and the roads were better than the ones near home. There were cars in Maroon Town, but they would pass by every now and again. In Kingston the cars just kept coming. We had to be very careful when we crossed the road. Living on the edge of a small place like Maroon Town the air was clean, but in the big city all the cars, all the people and all the animals created smells that I had never experienced. I was wondering if we smelt of country. I wiped the sweat off my forehead with my mum's sleeve and kept moving. We had our entire lives packed in one large, brown suitcase. Bits had fallen off it; the handle was just about hanging on. I tried to pick the suitcase up, but I couldn't even move it.

'My boy, you are not as strong as your dad yet,' my mum said smiling.

I felt sad. I felt useless. I wanted to help my mum but she peeled my fingers from the suitcase handle and carried it herself. When my dad wrote to Mum he would always write a line to me, telling me to be the man of the house while he was away, and here I was, being put in my place for trying to do as I was told. I dragged my feet and sulked as we weaved through the fruit markets and held our breaths through the meat section. I was terrified of Kingston; it was just so different from Maroon Town. People seemed hurried and stressed; their faces were wrinkled and less kind. We checked into a guest house near the port. There were two single beds, and as soon as I could I got into mine. I lay in bed unable to sleep for a long time because thoughts were rushing around my head about what the journey would be like. Outside, the noise of the city never seemed to stop. I started to think about my dad, I wanted to see him, of course, but I didn't want to leave the sunshine and I was already beginning to miss my grandma's arms.

The next morning was April 13, 1958. We quickly ate some fruit and rushed outside where we shuffled on to yet another broken old bus. As we approached the harbour, my attitude started to change. Many people were walking in the same direction and I could feel excitement in the air. Then, when I looked up, I saw the biggest thing I'd ever seen in my life: a ship!

Chapter Six

I stood on the harbour looking up at the ship, and I couldn't believe how big it was. It was taller than any building I have ever seen. Mainly black and white at the top, it was so big it partly blocked out the light. The front third of the ship had a big open deck, and the rest was covered. We waited in the long queue; it felt as if we were queuing for hours. The woman in front of us could not stop talking. She had two children with her, but she wasn't talking to them. One of the children, a girl, looked towards the ship expressionless, as if she didn't want to be there. I knew how she felt. The other, a slightly older girl, had her eyes fixed on her mum. I glanced up at my mum, but her eyes were fixed firmly on the queue in front and I could tell she was determined not to miss a step. It looked like she couldn't even breathe until we reached the desk at the front of the queue.

'Mum,' I said under my breath and pulling at her hand. 'Mum. Who is she talking to?'

'Just mind your own business, son,' replied Mum.

The woman was loud, but I couldn't understand why people around us were acting as if she wasn't there and carrying on as normal.

'But she's being so loud! Who's she talking to?'

'Jesus,' said Mum. 'She's talking to Jesus.'

We didn't go to church but we prayed sometimes, and I had never seen someone praying when waiting in a queue before.

'She's not eating. She's not going to sleep. She hasn't even got her eyes closed. Can you talk to Jesus like that?'

'The Lord move in mysterious ways,' Mum replied. 'And so do people. Now just quiet an' mind your own business.'

Finally, we reached the desk, and a big white man snatched a book that my mum was holding from her hand. His face was rigid and unfriendly. He wore a dark blue uniform, with a cap of the same colour. At the front of the cap there was what looked like two leaves, a gate and a crown. I hoped that not all white men were as stern and serious as him. He stamped my mum's book, gave it back to her and shooed us on. I turned and asked my mum who he was.

'Him is a customs officer. Him work for the Queen of England, and when you see people like him you must show them respect.'

My mum was the only queen I knew, indeed, her and my grandma were the only people on the earth who I truly respected. I couldn't understand why everything had become so stiff all of a sudden. Mum seemed nervous. She was rigid and looked uneasy.

We walked for a while, and then we came to the stairs that went up to the ship.

'Wow, it's so big. Is this the *Empire Windrush*?' I asked, feeling excited.

'No,' said Mum. 'De ship called *Arosa Star.*'

I noticed my mum holding on to a little blue book.

'What's that book?' I asked as we were walking up the steps.

'That is my passport,' she replied. She opened it and I could see a photo of her.

'Where's my passport?' I asked, feeling slightly annoyed and a little jealous.

'You don't need one,' she said.

'But why do you need one, and I don't?'

'The British government have said that you can't have one.'

'Why not?' I persisted.

'Because you're too young. I am British and

therefore, so are you.'

'But I am me, and you are you. I should have my own passport, shouldn't I?' I stopped halfway up the steps, blocking the way so that a queue of people formed behind me.

'Stop asking so many questions,' Mum said, taking my hand and tugging so that I'd keep walking. 'My passport is our passport. It promises us protection an' de freedom to travel in all British territories all over de world. That's what the Queen says, and if that's what de Queen says, that's de way it is, an' that's all you need to know.'

I stopped again, staring at the blue book. It looked important – and I wanted to feel important. I reached up and tried to pull my mum's passport from her hands, but she held it firmly. She frowned as she spoke to me, creating angry lines on her forehead.

'Stop it now. You're not to touch this, OK? If we lose this, then we can't ever see your dad again. Do you understand? So leave it.'

It was not very often I saw my mum so angry, and when she was I used to go for a walk in the bush, or I went to Grandma. Now there was nowhere to go, and Grandma wasn't there.

At the top of the stairs on the open deck, Mum put the suitcase down and took a couple of deep breaths.

There was another white man. He had a kinder face. He was dressed in a smart black uniform, but there was no crown on his cap. His had a small ship on it. I think he could see I was close to crying and Mum was tired, so he smiled at me and bent down to hand me a piece of paper.

'Do you need a hand with that suitcase, madam?' he asked.

'No,' said Mum. 'I'm OK.'

Then the man spoke to me.

'Now cheer up, little man,' he said. 'You're going to be fine. You see that paper there?'

I nodded and he continued. 'Well, on that paper you'll see the number of your cabin. It's a good cabin.' He pointed to some large doors. 'Just go through those doors, up the stairs to the second floor, and your cabin's starboard. That means on your right. And it's got a view, especially for you. You can see the sea day and night, and sometimes you can see other ships going by. Now that's not bad, is it?'

I nodded again.

'Right,' he continued. 'This is a great ship, so you'll have a good journey. I'll tell you what. If you don't have a *great* journey, I'll eat my hat.'

I could still feel the tears threatening to spill, but I smiled at the thought of him eating his hat.

'Thank you,' I said.

'It's my pleasure, little man.'

We went to the second floor and as we made our way along the corridor, I asked my mum why the second man didn't look at her passport.

'He doesn't work for the Queen. He works on the ship,' she replied. 'What does it say on the paper?'

I opened it up and read the words written there. 'Cabin 323.'

We walked around looking, and finally we reached our cabin. It was small. In one corner, it had a tiny bathroom with a shower with warm water. The walls were paper thin and when the woman on one side coughed, we could hear it as if she was in our room. On the other side there was a couple with a very small baby. I heard the baby crying, and it sounded like we were in one room altogether. But they must have been thinking that we sounded like we were in their room; the only difference was that I was no cry baby. But just like the nice man who worked on the ship said, we had a window, and when I climbed on the bed and looked through the window, I could see the sea, and the sea went on for ever.

As I looked out into the sea, Mum started to take things out of the suitcase. When she had done as much as she wanted to do, she lay on top of the bed. She was looking quietly at the ceiling, I was looking quietly at the sea, until we heard the engines start up with a big rumble, and voices shouting outside.

'Ship a leave.'

'We a leave now.'

'Forward to England.'

Mum jumped up off the bed and with much excitement said, 'Come, Leonard. Come, we go.'

I followed her downstairs to the deck, where it looked as if all the passengers had gathered. They were all talking and waving to the people on land. Mum's face lit up. Her mood changed and she was smiling. She found a place where we could see the people on the land.

'Wave,' she said. 'Wave to the people!'

I had no idea who I was waving to, but I did as my mum had said and waved. People were waving back so I waved more, and we didn't stop until our arms were heavy.

The ship slowly began to pull away and the people on deck started to go to their rooms. We returned to our cabin and I went back to the window where I could watch the people on land going away and the land getting smaller, and smaller. Mum was lying on the bed again. She looked tired, but I had to ask.

'Why were we waving to people we didn't know?'

'They are Jamaicans, son, and we're leaving them,' she said. 'But we not just waving to them; we waving to de country. We saying goodbye to Jamaica.'

Chapter Seven

When we were on our way, I asked Mum how long it would take to get to England. I knew this was going to be a long journey but when my mum told me it would take two weeks I jumped off my bed.

'Two weeks?' I said loudly.

'Look like you never hear me. Me tell you before, it will take a long, long time. You're lucky,' said Mum. 'Your dad took four weeks.'

'Why did he take so long?' I asked.

'Where's your postcard?' she asked. I took it out of my jacket pocket.

'Look carefully,' she said. 'The *Empire Windrush* is very big. Much bigger than this ship. So it was slower.'

I stared at the picture of Dad's ship, then I looked around the cabin. *Perhaps two weeks at sea could be fun*, I thought. There might be other kids to play with. We might see dolphins and sharks in the sea. We could even see a Great Whale. But then I thought of all the things that could go wrong. The other kids might not like me. I could get seasick, or homesick. I think the stress was showing on my face because Mum reached over to me, pinched my cheek, and smiled as she said, 'You saw what it's like. That's a very big sea out there. It goes a long way. I'm sure your dad is looking forward to seeing you. Are you excited to see him?'

'I don't know,' I said. 'I want to see him, but I'm going to miss Grandma.'

She pulled me towards her and whispered in my ear.

'Hey. Don't worry now. You're going to have such a wonderful life. You should know how lucky you are. Now go to the bathroom and change your clothes. It's time to relax!'

After we had both changed into more comfortable clothes, we out on to the deck where a band was playing some old-fashioned music. People were dancing and smiling and there was a sense of happiness in the air. The men were dressed in smart suits with big collars and baggy trousers. They wore white shirts with ties, and every one of them had a trilby hat. The women were wearing flowing, bright flowered frocks, with brightly coloured shoes, many with handbags to match, and ribbons or flowers in their hair. The deck was packed and we could hardly move. I noticed that the wind started getting stronger, and the waves in the sea were getting big. The ship was bouncing up and down and I started to feel dizzy. Then my mum kept on bopping up and down to the music, which just made it worse.

I was bored and the music and dancing didn't excite me. I could have more fun playing in our yard; I would be happier talking to Grandma. I was already beginning to miss her. I sat down in a chair at the edge of the dance floor. An old woman sat in the chair beside me, a cigarette clutched in her hand.

'What's the matter with you?' the old woman asked, leaning over. As she spoke smoke from the cigarette came out of her mouth. I could see my mum walking towards us.

'He's just tired,' my mum said having overheard the question. 'Him never realize how long the journey would be. He thinks he can't take two weeks of this, but I'm sure he can.'

'Ah, but now you have your whole life ahead of you. Yes, boy!' the old woman said. 'I could have only dreamt of going to England at your age. You're very lucky. You can get an education; you can work; you can do anything over there because you are going to the land of hope and glory.'

With a final wink, she danced off to join a group of people smoking and dancing in the middle of the deck. I didn't care about the land of hope and glory; all I wanted was my grandma.

It didn't take long for me to get used to the ship. Sometimes we ate in the big dining room, sometimes we had food in our room, but wherever we ate it, the food tasted disgusting. There was no Jamaican food, only dry chicken and plain boiled potatoes. Even my mum was finding it difficult to stomach the dryness. She winced and pouted her lips but kept telling me it was yummy as she ate, as if I was going to suddenly have a change of heart. It was horrible, and she knew it. I missed my sweet potatoes and yam. I missed my green bananas. I was really missing Grandma's cooking.

After a few days on board I met a boy around the same age as me. I first saw him when I was running around the ship deck not far from where he was sitting. He looked like a smaller version of the men on board. He wore a brown suit, shirt and tie, and he had a cap instead of a trilby. He wore black leather shoes that were so shiny that the sun reflected off them. He smiled at me and I smiled back. I was going to talk to him, but then woman who was sitting near to him saw me and she shouted at me, 'Leave him alone. He's studying.'

I ran away quickly. The next day I saw him again; he was in the same place, but this time he was on his own.

'What's your name?' I asked.

'Winston,' he replied.

'Why did your mum shout at me?'

'That's not my mum,' he said. 'That's my nanny.'

'Your grandma?' I asked. She had looked a bit young to be his grandma.

'No.'

'Your auntie?'

'No,' Winston replied, starting to laugh.

'Well, what kind of nanny is she?' I asked. I couldn't think of another relative you could call 'nanny'.

'She looks after me! I was born in England but sent back to Jamaica for a while to be raised by my uncle,' Winston explained. 'My uncle lives in a big house and is very busy, so Nanny's job is to look after all my clothes and make sure I eat at the right time. She teaches me, too. But now Nanny is taking me to England, where my mum and dad live.'

Suddenly he sat up straight and said, 'She's coming. You'd better go.'

I looked over my shoulder and saw Winston's nanny weaving through the crowds on the deck. I ran, but I didn't run far. I hid behind a big pillar and watched, as Winston opened a book she gave him, and he started to read aloud. His reading was good, but sometimes he would stop to ask her about a word, and then he would carry on. I sat and watched him for a while and once he looked up and saw me watching. He cracked a very quick smile, and from that moment I knew we were going to be friends.

Winston came from a rich family. His nanny could be quite strict, but he was allowed play times. There wasn't much for kids to do on the ship, and there weren't many kids, so all we did was walk around the ship and try to get lost. A couple of times we spoke to members of the ship's crew and they would give us sweets and tell us what it was like to be a sailor.

Sometimes there were church services on deck. My mum took me to one and there we prayed to God to take care of us on our journey. We made a few visits there, and one hot but windy day during a service, we were praying and a woman vomited all over her daughter. Most of the people just carried on praying but a man and a woman who were sitting next to them helped the lady and the girl.

'It's the food!' she shouted as she gasped for air. 'They're trying to kill us!'

'No,' said the man. 'This happens all the time. Is de way de ship roll.'

The girl began to sob.

'Don't worry,' said the lady. 'It's only de food.'

'You see, Mum,' I muttered. 'The food is not good.'

'God help us,' shouted the woman as the two helpers walked her and her daughter away to be cleaned up.

'It's not the food,' said Mum. 'She's just seasick, an' God help us all when we get to England.'

Chapter Eight

On Monday 28 April 1958, I woke up to the sound of people singing, as Mum shook me in my bed.

'Wake up, Leonard,' she said. 'Wake up! Come look.'

I was still in my pyjamas and she was wearing her night clothes, but she wasn't bothered. She took my hand and we rushed out on to the deck where a group of other passengers, some still in their night clothes too, were looking out into the distance. They were all chatting excitedly, pointing at a thin strip of land I could just about make out.

'That is England!'

'England, here we come!'

'De mother country.'

People started acting more frantically than ever, pushing past one another with excitement. The captain's voice came over the speaker system and could be heard all over the ship.

'This is your captain speaking. I am delighted to announce that in just under one hour we will be docking in the port of Southampton. I hope that you have enjoyed your journey. I, and the whole crew, would like to wish you all the best for your time in the United Kingdom. Please ensure that you have your papers ready for inspection when you leave the vessel.'

My mum took my hand and led me back to our cabin. We got washed and dressed, then bundled our belongings into the suitcase. Mum grabbed her passport and held it tightly.

'You should only speak to the English people when they speak to you, and you should do whatever they tell you to do,' she said.

I put the suit on that I wore when I boarded the ship – it was the only one that I had. Mum really got dressed up. She only ever dressed like this on special occasions. She wore high-heeled shoes, a pretty bright-red dress with a small red hat that sat to one side of her head. I couldn't understand why she was trying so hard to look good now. We were only getting off a ship.

We waited for a while with the suitcase packed and placed next to the door, until we began to feel the ship slowing down. Then, for the first time in two weeks, we stopped moving. We rushed to the deck and waited in line to leave the ship. It felt like we were there for hours, moving slowly, step by step until we got to the stairs. At the top were two men wearing the uniforms that meant they worked for the Queen. Mum handed her passport to one of the men; he looked at it, stamped a page, and then gave it back. He looked at me.

'I don't have a passport,' I said.

'That's all right, young man,' he said. 'Don't worry. You're one of us now. You'll have your own passport when you grow up.'

As we went down the steps I had to hold on to the handrail because Mum had to take the suitcase by herself, and it looked difficult. I just wished I was big enough to help her. Below, I could see a crowd had gathered. There were newspaper reporters, their pens and papers at the ready, and even people with television cameras. As we got off the ship and walked on to the dock, the cold hit me. It was freezing, and my suit was not warm enough for the English weather! I felt the chill run all the way down my spine. I took my first sharp intake of English air. It tasted different. Mum quickly whipped out a blanket from our case and wrapped it around my shoulders, just as we were approached by a television reporter. He was a small, stocky white man, wearing a big warm coat.

'Excuse me, can I ask you why you've come to England?' he asked loudly, the camera in our faces.

My mum halted and turned to him, respectfully. 'I have come to see my husband and to make a better life for my child, sir.'

'Could you not have made a good life for your child back home then, miss?' the man responded.

'I have come to help my husband, rebuild the mum country, and to give my child the opportunity to grow and prosper.'

My mum's voice had changed. She was trying her best to sound English. I couldn't understand why she was speaking the way she did, and why we were being asked so many questions.

'Do you think that you'll fit into life in England then, miss?' the man continued, bringing the camera even closer to our faces. 'Your child might find it difficult looking like that.' The man gestured towards my blanket.

'He's not used to the English weather and our clothes are all neatly packed in preparation to start rebuilding the mother country, sir. England is part of Britain, and Jamaica is part of Britain, so we are excited to meet more British people and to rebuild the motherland.'

The reporter nodded and swiftly and moved on to interrogate someone else.

In Jamaica we didn't have television yet, but I knew

it was full of famous white people. So I wondered if having just arrived in England, I was now a famous black boy. I looked back and saw that he was talking to everyone he could and I realized that we can't all be famous, but it was nice to know that I could be on television. Even if I was just looking cold.

Chapter Nine

We walked away from the ship, and I got colder and colder. The cold felt as if it was going deep into me. The port was much bigger than the one in Kingston, and not far from our ship there was another with people getting on. Some people were hugging and kissing their loved ones goodbye, and others were moving around pushing boxes on trollies or carrying suitcases. It was busy. We walked around, then suddenly Mum stopped. She looked at me, shrugged her shoulders, and asked, 'Leonard. You can see any coach?'

'What's a coach?'

'Is like a bus. Same ting. You see any bus?'

'No,' I replied looking around as much as I could.

I kept looking around and Mum sat on the suitcase. She looked out into the distance as if lost. Then I looked up to the sky and saw the sun shining.

'Look,' I said. 'The sun is shining.'

'Of course it is,' replied Mum.

I was really confused. 'How do they do that?'

'Do what?'

'How do they have sunshine when it's so cold?'

Mum laughed. 'The sun shines in cold places as well as hot places. The sun gives light as well as heat. You can't have everything.'

A man in uniform noticed us sitting there and began walking over.

'Can I be of help to you, madam?' he asked as he reached us.

'Yes,' said Mum, looking relieved. 'We need to get de coach to de train station; can you tell me where it is please, sir?'

'Of course,' he said. 'I'll do better than that – I'll take you there. Come on, let me carry your suitcase.'

He took the suitcase in his hand and we headed to the bus together.

'So, what's your name?' he asked me as we walked.

'Leonard,' I replied.

'Now that's a good name. Leonard,' he said, as if trying it out. 'So, young Leonard, what do you want to do when you grow up?'

'I want to be like my grandma.'

'Oh. What does your grandma do?'

'She's does kindness. She's kind to everyone.'

'Now that's a good answer. We should all be kind.'

Mum looked at me and smiled, and as we reached the bus I looked again at his uniform – it was different from any of the men on the ship.

'Are you a policeman?' I asked.

'No.'

'Are you a sailorman?'

'No.'

'Are you the bus driver?'

'No.'

'So what kind of job do you do?' I asked, running out of ideas.

'I do this,' he replied, lifting the suitcase up higher. 'I am a porter.'

'What does a porter do?' I asked.

'Kindness,' he said with a big smile on his face. 'I try to be kind to everyone.'

As we boarded the coach, for the first time since we'd left Jamaica I began to feel excited about seeing my dad. I wondered what adventures he'd had, whether he'd made any friends and if he was excited to see me too.

I was cold to the bone and I could see my mum's teeth chattering. The coach was packed with people, but we found seats near the front. I recognized some makes of cars because I saw them in Jamaica, but there were lots of cars that I had never seen before. Looking out of the window I saw people walking fast in big coats. They all looked like that had somewhere to go or something to do. The houses and shops were packed together, very little or no space in between them, and it looked grey compared to the green everywhere of Maroon Town.

When we got off the coach at the train station another porter took us to the train for Manchester. I could see from the signs that some people were travelling to Birmingham, some to London and some to Sheffield. I found it incredibly confusing as many of these place names were the same as place names in Jamaica.

'Mum,' I said as we walked behind the porter, 'did you see those places? Cambridge, Falmouth, Kingston. They just like Jamaica.'

'That's right, son,' Mum replied. 'When the British were in Jamaica, they named places after the ones they left behind. They did it everywhere they went.'

'Are there coconut trees, yams, or sweet potatoes here?'

'Yes,' said Mum.

'Great!' I said.

'Them nu grow here. They get them from Jamaica.'

Then we were at the train. The porter lifted the suitcase up to us and we said goodbye.

'Cheerio,' said the porter. 'And welcome to England.'

I had never been on a train before. It had a strange smell – a mixture of wood and cigarettes. We found some seats, and soon the train was moving out. But as we started moving, I saw Winston and his nanny waiting on the platform for another train. I tried to call to him, but Mum said I must not shout. So I waved my hands just in case he could see me, but he didn't, and then we were gone. I was a little upset, but I didn't want to show it. Although I'd only known him for two weeks, it was really sad not to say goodbye properly.

As the train was moving I began to get a bit warmer. It was great to be going past everything outside so quickly. I wanted to walk around the train, but Mum said that I had to sit still and behave. I couldn't understand why she had become so stiff and rigid suddenly.

'Keep still, Leonard,' she said. 'Do you want these English people to think you're out of control? You must be respectful.'

'I don't like it here,' I said.

'You don't know what you like or don't like. You haven't even been here a day!'

I pulled away from her and started staring out of

the window. I missed my grandma more than ever. *She wouldn't like it here*, I thought. The cities looked so crowded, and the houses were close together. The sun was shining, but everything was so grey. Before I got on the train, I noticed that people everywhere seemed to be smoking, but even on the train people were smoking. They coughed and spluttered all the time. As the train moved deeper into the countryside, I began to see little white dots, which I soon realized were sheep. Then I saw cows, and then we were back in a city again.

The journey was like that all the way. Countryside, countryside, town or city, countryside, countryside, town or city. Mum kept falling asleep and waking up, falling asleep and waking up, and I was just watching people. Most of the people on the train were not talking, they were reading newspapers. Many of the women were wearing coats and pretty hats, like the hats women wore in Jamaica when they were going to church. The men were wearing coats or suits, and round hats. Everyone looked very serious. There were two men in front of us that I don't think were together because they didn't speak to each other, but they were dressed exactly the same and they both had a copy of the same newspaper. Now and then, they glanced at me and Mum over the top of their papers. I looked away, pretending I couldn't see them.

Chapter Ten

We arrived at London Road Station in Manchester in the early evening. A woman that I recognized from the ship helped my mum carry her case off the train. Mum looked towards the station exit, and a big smile spread across her face. I followed her gaze and saw a man smiling back, walking towards us. I knew it had to be my dad. He was wearing a long, heavy coat and although I'd seen photos, I barely recognized him. He looked as stiff as the coat that clung to him. I tried to smile back but my face felt stiff. In photographs that I saw of him taken before I was born, he had looked so relaxed, basking in the sunlight with my mum, his skin shining, his eyes bright and wide with happiness. The man in front of me looked so different.

He reached us and swept me into a tight hug. I stared at him, but I just didn't feel like I knew him. Even his smell was strange. Hugging him was nothing like hugging Grandma, so I pushed him away.

'Hey. You don't give you dad a hug?' he said. 'Anyway. Good to see you. Long time now me want see you.' His eyes were excited. Mine were not.

My mum laughed and replied, 'He's just tired, my dear. It's been the longest journey.'

'It's OK, he'll get used to me,' said my dad as he patted me lightly on the head. I hoped that was true and that I would get used to him. I knew that he loved me and I felt guilty for not liking him more. But I couldn't fake it.

We walked through the city centre and suddenly, although I knew they weren't really, it felt like everyone's eyes were on me. It felt like people were stopping and whispering about me, pointing in our direction and tutting at me. I felt like I had entered another world. There was so much concrete. So many buildings packed together. People walked quickly. No one seemed to be just out enjoying themselves. They were all going to, or coming from, somewhere.

When we reached the house, I couldn't believe what I saw. I remembered Mum saying that dad had come to England to make a 'better life for us' but this didn't look better. The front of the house was close to where people walked. There was a house either side of it, and it went up, and not across. Then Dad told me that we didn't have the house to ourselves. We went inside and

I was shocked to see that we were to live in one room with mouldy walls, and a carpet so old it was sticking to my shoes as I walked. There was a big bed and a settee. My dad showed me how it folded down into a bed with such pride, but in all honesty, I didn't care about fold-down beds. I wanted to swing from coconut trees and graze my knees against the bark. The settee was mine, right next to the paraffin heater and next to a small table. My dad then extended a cloth partition saying proudly, 'And this, my son, is how you turn one room into two rooms.'

I didn't want to say anything to hurt his feelings, but I couldn't help myself. I said, 'No. This is just one room with a partition.'

My parents glanced at each other. They didn't say anything, and because they didn't say anything I thought they knew I was telling the truth. 'I had my own room in Jamaica. I could play outside in the sun. I could eat fruit whenever I wanted to; the food was sweet; there was lots of space – inside and outside. I want to go home!'

'Be patient, my child,' my dad replied. 'Things will get better, I promise.'

But I wasn't finished. I looked around at the poky flat, at the concrete buildings outside the window and the cold grey sky beyond. 'You've been here for a long time. In all your letters you say you are taking care of things and doing well, but this is all you've got.'

My mum yanked my arm towards her and looked straight into my eyes.

'Your dad is trying his best for us,' she said. 'Do you know how lonely it must have been for him over here? These things take time. He's breaking his back so that you can live good. Lord help you and your selfishness. I didn't raise you to be so spoilt.'

I looked at my dad's face – his eyes were lowered to the floor and he looked even more disheartened than when I pushed him away at the station. I didn't cry aloud, but the tears I'd been trying to hold back since we left Jamaica rolled down from my eyes. I was feeling guilty again. Everyone wanted to help me, but I didn't know if I needed help. I knew what I wanted.

'I'm sorry, Dad,' I said. 'I just miss Grandma.'

He came and sat next to me on the bed, like a king on his throne, and smiled at me like he smiled in those photographs. I felt connected to him for the first time.

'I know it's scary moving to a new place,' he said. 'I was scared too, when I came over on that big ship, de *Empire Windrush* – scared an' lonely. I had no one except—' He stopped and glanced at Mum. Then he carried on. 'I had no one, except... except myself. But it nu matter now. Now this is our home an' soon we will live in a palace like de Queen and King of England, my child.'

'OK,' I said. He stroked my head tenderly. I closed my eyes and let the tears roll.

He stopped stroking my head and wiped the tears off my cheeks.

'Everything will be fine,' he said. 'Everything will be fine.'

I tried to imagine what fine meant for a moment, and I couldn't, so I just said, 'This is not better than Jamaica.'

Chapter Eleven

I found life hard in that room. There were suitcases everywhere, and I wasn't allowed to play in the garden. Our family weren't even allowed to go into the garden. We had to share the kitchen and the bathroom with people living in the other rooms, and so we weren't allowed to even keep things in the kitchen and the bathroom to avoid problems. Whenever we went to the kitchen, my mum would weigh me down with pots and pans. Sometimes they were piled up above my head. One day I walked head-first into a large, white man with brown teeth who growled at me like he was a bear. I went back to our room and sulked. I sulked for a while until Mum stood in front of me and said, 'Cheer up, Leonard. Never mind that man.' She smiled. The smile got bigger and bigger. 'Me have something for you.'

Then I noticed that she had her hands behind her back. I wasn't sure what treat she had to cheer me up.

'What you have there?' I asked.

'A letter from Grandma,' she said, quickly handing the letter to me.

I grabbed the letter. It came in a bigger letter that was sent to Mum and Dad. Mum began to read the one she had, and I read mine. Grandma wrote in big capital letters.

DEAR LEONARD,

I HOPE YOU ARE DOING FINE. I AM VERY WELL HERE, BUT I MISS YOU A LOT. SOMETIMES I THINK I CAN HEAR YOU PLAYING BALL OUTSIDE, BUT IT'S JUST ME.

WE HAD A SMALL HURRICANE THE OTHER DAY, BUT IT WASN'T TOO BAD. IT COME AND GONE NOW.

I JUST WANT YOU TO BE GOOD OVER THERE. DO THE BEST YOU CAN AT SCHOOL, AND WALK GOOD.

TAKE CARE, AND MAY GOD BLESS YOU. YOUR GRANDMOTHER.

After a week of us all living in the room, Dad had been given permission by the bus company to take two weeks off work to be with us, and I was grateful for that. I didn't get to know him when he was working, because I only saw him for a short time in the morning before he left for work, and a short time when he came home. I thought that he must have felt the same too because I kept talking about how much I missed Maroon Town. I hated those first nights sleeping on the bed-settee. It wasn't anywhere near as comfortable as my bed in Jamaica. It was always cold and I just kept waking up in the night.

I also found the food really strange. We had lots of Jamaican food like sweet potatoes, yam, ackee and saltfish. We had callaloo, breadfruit and mangoes, but they tasted different. At least the food in Manchester was better than the food on the ship.

I started going for walks with Mum and Dad, and when they started to take me shopping I found out where they were getting the Jamaican food from. They actually had Jamaican shops in Manchester. Some were owned by Jamaicans, but some were owned by Asians.

I began to understand why people walked so fast in England. It was to keep warm. Copying them, I began to walk fast when I was cold, and it worked! Well, it helped. If I walked fast in Jamaica, I would get too hot and tired, but in Manchester it made sense. The city was noisy and busy. There were pubs on many of the street corners, factories with smoke coming from their chimneys, and large cinemas, but the tallest buildings of all were the churches. Down the side streets children played on the road, and dogs roamed freely. I began getting used to it but it felt nothing like the freedom of sprinting through the trees of Maroon Town, or running around the palm trees only to come home and tumble into my grandma's embrace. I couldn't complain. I didn't want to upset my parents any more, so I kept my feelings to myself. I thought of my grandma's words; 'Lions always roar.' I wanted to roar louder than ever before.

Everywhere that I went, Mum or Dad were always with me; I couldn't go out and play freely like I used to. I saw cats and dogs in Manchester, but I missed the goats, the lizards, the mongooses, and the hummingbirds of Jamaica. I missed all the wild animals I used to chase when they were not chasing me. After a while I got used to staying indoors and began to prefer it because the white people couldn't stare at us there.

It was strange to see young people and children just walking past elders and not saying good morning or good evening. In Jamaica, in the area where I lived, we kids always had to say hello to the elders. If we didn't, the message would reach home, sometimes before we got there ourselves. If I forgot, the elder I'd ignored would tell my mum, 'Your son pass me this morning and never bother say hello.' Then when I got home there would be trouble.

Kids did play out on the street where we were living, but they never spoke to me. I didn't see much of the neighbours, and I never saw Mum or Dad talk to them or anyone else living on our road either. Most people seemed to get on with each other on the street, but they weren't getting on with us. And we just happened to be the only black family on the street.

One day, Dad came home and when he opened the door he shouted, 'Catch.' I turned to see him walking in through the door with a new football in his hand. He tossed it to me, and I caught it.

'Me have to go back to work tomorrow,' he said. 'So, let's make de most of me last day off an' go to de park and kick some ball. What you say?'

I grinned at him. I hadn't been in England long and I hadn't seen much. The room, the Jamaican shop, a few sights around the city, Central Library, the cathedral, the Corn Exchange and Albert Square, but up until then we did nothing that was just fun. We had walked past parks, but never gone into one.

'OK,' I said enthusiastically. 'Let's go.'

Mum said she'd never kicked a ball, and she never would, so Dad and I left for the park, just the two of us. As we walked we bounced the ball between us. It was a warm day. Not hot, but the warmest day since I had been in England.

As soon as we entered the park and we were at the edge of the grass play area, dad threw the ball in the air and kicked it as far as he could. He started running after the ball.

He can run! I thought, staring after him for a moment. Then I sprinted to catch up.

'You're fast, but not that fast,' I said as I passed him, and I kept going until the ball was at my feet. It was now his job to get the ball off me.

Dad was relaxed, and I really did need to stop thinking about life in Jamaica or life in England, and just play. He tried to get the ball, but I dribbled, and dribbled. Every time his feet came near me, I did some trickery and got away from him. Then as he stood in front of me, desperate to find a way of outsmarting me he pointed over my left shoulder and shouted, 'What is that?' I turned to see what it was, and he took the ball.

'You cheat,' I shouted.

'That's not cheating,' he said running away from me with the ball at his feet. 'You have the ball, so you shouldn't lose concentration. Just like I was concentrating on getting the ball. You should concentrate on keeping it.'

He laughed, knowing he was right, I smiled, knowing he was right, and then he kicked the ball back to me. I thought about challenging him to take it off me again, but in the spirit of good sportsmanship I passed it back to him. And so we continued. He would move towards a space, I would kick it into the space, and then he would do the same for me.

We stopped running around when we both started to run out of energy, and instead of passing into spaces we were moving at walking pace and passing to each other's feet.

'Let's go,' called Dad. 'I think we both need a drink.'

As we were walking towards the park gate he put his arm around me. My mind went back to when me and Mum arrived at the train station, and how I didn't like his touch. Now this felt different. It felt loving. It felt warm. He felt like my dad for the first time.

'You're not a bad player,' he said. 'Did you play football in Maroon Town?'

'Me and my friends kick a ball around sometimes, but we never had proper games. But I like football.'

'Well, if you like football, this is the place to be. They had a great team here,' he said as we walked down the street. 'But you know in life sometimes things don't go to plan. Sometimes everything is going good, then everything goes bad. There is a football team here called Manchester United, this year they were climbing to the top of the table. In February, they went abroad and beat the best team in Yugoslavia, so things were going great. But on the way back, their plane crashed, and twenty-three people died; eight of them were players. It's a real shame.'

'That's horrible,' I said. I thought about how great the team would have felt when they won that game, but how badly it ended. I wondered how difficult it must have been for those that lived.

'Yes. It was terrible,' Dad replied. 'Like I said, things can be going great, then suddenly everything changes. That's why you should be thankful for every day, and never take a day or a person for granted.' He held my hand slightly tighter as we walked. 'You don't know what that day will bring, and you don't know how long someone you love will be around.'

He sounded very serious, but then he looked at me and smiled.

'Is the football team still going?' I asked.

'Yes. They say they will rebuild and come back even stronger.'

I must have looked really worried because suddenly he stopped.

'Are you OK?' he asked.

'Yes,' I said. 'I just don't know if I ever want to fly or play football in the future.'

'You don't have to do either,' he said. 'But you must understand that almost everything in life has risks. You just have to know that if you get knocked down you must pick yourself up and try again. Never give up.'

Chapter Twelve

All that football had made me thirsty and my stomach was rumbling too. As we walked back home, on a corner of the high street I spotted a shop selling food and drinks. It was a small, colourful shop, and one window displayed lots of sweets and cakes. I stopped Dad and nodded towards the shop. Dad just shook his head.

'Sorry, son. We can't go in there.'

'Why not? Those cakes look nice, and they have soft fruit drinks.'

'They have a colour bar there,' Dad said still shaking his head.

'What's a colour bar?' I asked.

My dad used his arm that was still around my shoulder and guided me closer to the door. With his other hand he pointed to a hand-written notice on the door:

SORRY. WE DON'T SERVE COLOUREDS

HERE.

'What are coloureds?' I asked.

'That's what they call us,' he replied. 'They call us coloured because of our skin,'

'So we can't go in?'

'No. But don't worry about that. There are other places.'

We walked for less than a minute when we came to another shop selling drinks where we entered and bought a cake each and some fruit juice in glass bottles. We began to eat as we walked, then we walked into a church yard and sat down on a bench.

'If we call ourselves black people, why do they call us coloured?' I asked, still puzzled by the sign.

'There are some white people who think that white is de best, de standard, and everyone else is coloured. And because they think they are the best, they think they have de right to rule over us. You know 'bout slavery?'

'Yes,' I replied.

'Well, some people still think like they did back then. They can't keep us in slavery any more, but they still want to control us.'

'But can they do that?' I asked.

'Put it like this, son, there's no law stopping them. Now, you see the shop where we got this food?'

'Yes.'

'Good. So remember that there are also good people here.'

'But that is so bad.'

'I know, but listen to this. Right now, in the United States, there are signs on benches like this one. Some say 'For whites only', some say 'For coloureds only'. The buses, shops, trains and even toilets are separated into white and coloured areas. So think about that. They are even killing black people over there.'

'Does that happen over here?'

Dad thought for a while. 'It's not the same here, but people have been attacked, and a few times me and some friends had to run for our lives.'

I felt frightened. 'Really?'

'Yes.' He looked at me sharply. 'Don't tell your mum. I don't want to worry her, but sometimes the nights here can be dangerous. These attacks usually happen at night.'

I finished my cake and drink. We put our rubbish in the bin and stood up.

'In the nights we have to look out for the bad people,' he said. 'In the day we just have to look out for the colour bar.'

'I hate that word,' I said. 'Coloured.'

'I know,' said Dad, putting his arm around my

shoulder again and leading me out. 'I know. They call us coloured, as if our colour changes, but we born black, we stay black, an' we die black. We don't turn purple; we don't turn blue or red. We're just black. So never be ashamed of that, son, you hear me. No matter what anyone else calls you, you are black. Never be ashamed of that.'

Chapter Thirteen

My dad had to go back to work driving buses, but he began to take me to the park to play football often, and I loved it. Sometimes he took me to work and I would just sit on the bus until my dad took me home, or my mum would get on at a bus stop, and then take me home. I used to enjoy seeing the city, listening to the way people spoke and the things they talked about. My mum was getting more confident travelling around Manchester. She was always reading about life in England, and she started going shopping alone. She loved the dresses that the ladies wore, so she spent a lot of time window shopping, and when she had money she would treat herself to a new dress and shoes. She also started looking for a school for me to attend, and before long she found me a place at Hyde Primary school.

I only had to go to primary school for a few months before the summer, then one more year, and I'd be going up to secondary school, but I was very nervous. It would be hard starting somewhere where I knew nobody. I imagined the school would be even stricter than Jamaican schools, and the building would be cold. The school wasn't very far from where we lived, and the day before I started my mum took me to meet the head teacher. His name was Mr Walsh. He showed my mum and me around the school hurriedly, and barely looked at us when he spoke. The children were all having lessons and the first thing I noticed was that none of them looked Jamaican, and none of them wore a school uniform. Upon leaving, we turned to Mr Walsh to say goodbye, and in reply he just warned us that I always had to be on time, and that bad attendance was not tolerated. He forced himself to smile for a split second and said, 'Goodbye now.'

The next day, my mum walked me to school for my first day. At the school gate we were met by a teacher. Her name was Miss Bright, and she was bright. Her clothes were bright, and her smile was bright, and she looked so happy to see me: the complete opposite of the head teacher. She knew my name, and she told Mum that I was going to be fine at school, and that all children were nervous on their first day, so she said I wasn't to worry. But I was worried. Miss Bright was fine, but the building was scary. The school was big, the walls were high, and when people spoke, the sound bellowed all around. My mum left me with Miss Bright, and although she was friendly, I felt alone. Miss Bright took me to the head teacher's office. Mr Walsh, the head teacher told me to wait outside his office, and then Miss Bright went.

I waited outside the office alone, and instead of feeling more relaxed I felt more nervous. Eventually the bell rang, then Mr Walsh came marching out.

'Follow me,' he said.

I walked with him until suddenly we were in the assembly hall, and there I was, standing with the head teacher in front of over a hundred children. I saw Miss Bright was sitting to the side with some other teachers, then Mr Walsh spoke. His voice filled the room and everyone listened.

'Children, today we have a new pupil, Leonard. Leonard has travelled here all the way from Jamaica. It's very hot there. We haven't got any children here from Jamaica so if there's anything you want to know about Jamaica, just ask Leonard. As always, I want you all to be on your best behaviour, and I want you to set a good example for him.'

I saw a hundred children looking at me, and all I could do was look at them. I watched as a couple of students on the front row nudged each other, holding back laughter. I joined the front row and they sang a hymn. I felt as if my voice had gone and I wanted to disappear. Then I remembered something.

'Lions always roar,' I muttered to myself. Then I just started singing. I don't know what I was singing. I just tried to make noises that sounded like the noises everyone else was making.

I was taken from the hall to a class that had about thirty children. They had all been in the assembly but as soon as I went in I was told by Miss Bright to introduce myself again.

'Hello,' I said. 'My name is Leonard.'

The children buckled with laughter and I felt my face grow hotter. I continued.

'I come from a very nice place called Maroon Town, it in Jamaica. I am ten years old.'

The giggles started up again.

'Stop it,' said Miss Bright sharply, and the giggles cut off. As soon as she spoke the class sat up straight and went quiet.

'Thank you, Leonard,' she said. 'Maroon Town sounds lovely. Why don't you go and sit down at that empty seat there.' I sat down where she had pointed, next to a tall boy who glanced at me, but didn't smile. As the class went on, I realized just how good a teacher Miss Bright was. She would say funny things and make the whole class laugh, but when she was serious there was no laughing and everyone listened.

When lunchtime came, I walked slowly into the playground with my head down. I could feel the heat of the eyes on me. I just wanted to find a corner to shrink into. A boy came up to me and tapped me on the shoulder, which startled me. When I looked around I recognized the boy from my class.

'Is Jamaica in Africa?' he asked.

'No. It ina de Caribbean. Far from Africa,' I said.

'Does everyone out there look like you then?' he asked. I noticed he was looking at my hair.

'No. Most people do. But there are Indian people, Chinese people, all kinds of people.'

'Chinese people don't have hair like yours, do they?'

'Is that why the other children were laughing? Because of my hair?'

'I don't know,' he replied. 'Miss Bright told us that there was going to be a coloured boy coming to the school, and she told us what your hair was like, but she didn't tell us that you would sound like that. They're laughing because of your voice.'

'What's wrong with my voice?' I asked. I never thought my voice was anything of interest before; no one had ever questioned the way I spoke. My grandma had always told me that I had a 'beautiful voice'.

'They've never heard anyone talk like you before,' he said.

'What is your name?' I asked, trying to change the subject. So now people thought I was strange because of the sound of my voice, as well as the colour of my skin!

'Mark. Let's go and get some food.'

The food was served in the big hall where we had the morning assembly. We waited in line and when it was our turn to be served, the dinner ladies slapped some mashed potato on to our plates, along with a piece of meat and some green peas, then she covered it all with gravy. We sat down and picked at our food. Seeing that Mark didn't look like he was loving his meal, I asked, 'Do you like the food at school?'

'Of course not,' he said. 'No one likes school dinners, and if you do, you shouldn't tell anyone.'

'Why not?'

'Because it's school. We eat it all up and then we say we don't like it. I feel sorry for the people who cook it.'

'Why?'

'Because – look at all the children here. It's hard to cook and make everyone happy.'

'You're right,' I said as I thought about the people who had to cook for all the people on the ship. 'I never thought about that.'

After a while more children began to speak to me, but they were always asking questions.

'Where do you come from?'

'Where is Jamaica?'

'Are there houses in Jamaica?'

'How do you wash your hair?'

'How do you wash your face?'

'Can you play cricket?'

'Do you eat bananas?'

'Can you sing?'

'Can you dance?'

'Can I touch you?'

To start with, I had a lot of those kinds of questions at Hyde Primary school. But my classmates did get used to me after a while. I understood that they had not had a Jamaican at the school before, but they were always asking me strange questions that I couldn't answer. I got tired of it, but I tried to be polite. Sometimes I wondered if they really liked me, or were they just pretending to like me. Or maybe they talking to me because I was strange to them, and they had never spoken to anyone like me. I just got fed up of telling them that I didn't know what the capital of Africa was.

Chapter Fourteen

Just as I was getting used to the school and the other children, and they were getting used to me, we broke up for the long summer holiday. People were talking about how hot the summer could be, but it didn't feel hot to me. The sun shone sometimes, but it never really got hot. It rained a lot too, but unlike in Jamaica where, after rain, there was heat to dry up all the puddles, here there was no heat so it always felt damp. The death of the footballers had affected the whole country, the weather was affecting the whole country, so people were saying 1958 was a bad year, with a bad summer.

I still hadn't made any friends. I used to talk to Mark and a couple of other people at school, but any time I suggested meeting up after school they always made excuses; some of them even said their parents wouldn't like me. Strange, because I never suggested meeting up with their parents.

Dad bought a small black-and-white television

for us which I spent a lot of time watching that wet summer. What I saw on television made me realize why the children at school laughed at my accent. My accent was nothing like theirs and nothing like the people I saw on television. I thought that on television I would see and hear people like me, but there were none. If there were any black people, they were always American, and if it was a film they would always be servants or bad people.

On one of her shopping trips, Mum met another Jamaican woman called Maud. We weren't related, but I had to call her Aunt Maud anyway. She had been in England a couple of years and was working as a nurse. She was married, but had no children, and just like Mum she liked shopping too, so they began to spend a lot of time together. Sometimes Aunt Maud would come over to our house for dinner, or for a cup of tea. I liked seeing her, and she always made Mum happy when they were together.

Sometimes, instead of watching television, I'd jump on the bus to keep Dad company. He drove the same bus route all the time though, so I started to get bored of riding it with him. When he had time off he would take me around Manchester and to the park for a kickaround. Mum and Dad said I should start going out to try to make new friends. I just think they wanted to spend more time on their own. So I began to go for walks in the park and around the streets, on my own. It was a great way to get to know the city. When I saw gangs of white kids, I would get nervous, but then I remembered, I am a Maroon, and I felt stronger. Sometimes when I saw other black kids, I would want to go to speak to them, but I didn't know what to say. I couldn't just go up to them and say, 'Hello, I'm black too. How did you come here?', so I just kept myself to myself. It was a damp summer, but I was learning a lot about England and its people. Then just a few days before I had to go back to school, I learned a lot more.

I was in the park, kicking the ball around by myself. It had rained that morning so the ground was soggy, but the sun had now come out and it was warming up. Not far away there were a group of boys also playing football.

I'm always playing on my own, I thought, watching as one of the boys scored an epic goal and his friends cheered. It would be great to play with them. I wasn't brave enough to go over and ask to join in, but a couple of minutes later I thought my opportunity had come. One of them had kicked the ball too far and it was coming in my direction. I left my ball, ran over to theirs and kicked it back. One of the boys trapped the ball with his foot before picking it up. The boys glanced at each other, then they started coming over to me. I noticed there were seven of them, so with me, we could make four a side.

'We can play,' I called as they came nearer.

'We don't play with blacks,' the boy with the ball shouted back at me. 'And who told you that you could touch my ball?'

It was only when they were standing in front of me that I realized how angry they were.

'I'm sorry,' I said. 'I just want to pass it back to save you from coming all de way over here.'

'Well, we're here now,' said the biggest boy there. He looked so angry I didn't want to look at him too long. Then the boy with the ball continued.

'Why don't you go down to Notting Hill? We don't want you around here, you dirty, stupid golliwog.'

I could see a couple of them trying to circle me, but I was busy trying to make sense of what the boy with the ball was saying.

'What is Notting Hill?' I asked.

'You know, it's where you lot are causing trouble. We don't want you up here.'

The next thing I felt was an arm around my neck. One of the boys had jumped me and was choking me. I thought about fighting back, but I knew I stood no chance against seven of them, and as he squeezed me I could feel myself getting weak. I couldn't breathe. Then he pushed me to the ground. I curled up in a ball to protect myself. A couple of them kicked me, and then they started throwing mud at me.

'Go back to Notting Hill,' they kept shouting. 'We don't want you round here.'

Finally, they left, running out of the park before anyone spotted what they'd done. I stayed curled up for a few moments, until I was sure they weren't coming back. I opened my eyes, then I straightened my legs and my neck, and looked around. When I could see that they really had gone I stood up. My arms and legs hurt where they had kicked me, and my clothes, face and hair were covered in mud. I looked for my ball, but it had gone.

As I walked home, I lowered my head so I didn't have to make eye contact with anyone. When I came through the front door, Mum gasped and ran over.

'What them do to you? Let me call de police. Oh Lord. Who them is? Them is wicked people.'

They might have been wicked, but I didn't want to call the police because I didn't want them to come looking for me after.

'I'm OK, Mum.' I said. 'Don't bother wid police. I don't know who they are. They ran away. I just need a bath.'

After my bath, my mum was trying to do everything she could for me.

'Do you want something to eat?'

'No.'

'Do you want to sleep for a while?'

'No. I'm not tired.'

'Where's your ball?'

'They took it.'

'Don't worry,' she said. 'I'll get you another one.'

'What is Notting Hill, Mum?' I asked.

'Why?'

'When the boys were hitting me, they kept telling me to go back to Notting Hill.'

My mum started looking around the room. She couldn't see what she was looking for so then she started walking around the room, until she saw a bit of her newspaper popping out from underneath the bed. She picked it up and turned the front page towards me.

RACE RIOTS IN NOTTING HILL. WAR ON THE STREETS .

'Where is Notting Hill?' I asked.

'It's in London,' Mum replied. 'And it's not a riot. The white people attacked the black people. That is racism, not a race riot. The only thing black people can do is defend themselves.'

'I don't understand,' I said. 'If there are shops that

won't serve us, places we can't go, children that beat up black children, adults that beat up black adults, why do we stay here? Why do any black people stay here? They don't want us here.'

Mum came over to my bed and sat next to me. She rubbed my back, just like she used to do when I was a baby.

'The first thing you must remember is that you are a Maroon. You come from a long line of freedom fighters, and we Maroons have never surrendered. Then you must understand. We have the right to be here. I have a British passport, your dad has a British passport, and you are a British subject. There is an organization called the White Defence League; all they want to do is get us out of this country. Not all white people are like them, but we have to let them know that we shall not be moved. We cannot give up.'

When my dad came home and saw me, he was angry. He told us that black people had also been attacked in Nottingham, and he was worried that things might get worse in Manchester. I thought about the way Jamaicans had to fight for their freedom, then I thought about what was happening to black people in England, and I wondered if we really could stay here. I was worried about me, and I was worried about Mum and Dad.

Chapter Fifteen

I started to see reports on the television about people being beaten up on the streets because of the colour of their skin. There were people talking about sending us all back home. I started to realize just how much discrimination was happening in the country, and it shocked me. I thought that big people should know better. Sometimes I asked questions about the things I saw on television, sometimes I didn't.

One Sunday, just before I went back to school, I could feel some tension at home. When I tried to talk to my parents, they answered without saying much. I thought they had argued over me, but didn't want me to know. After about an hour of sitting silently watching television, Mum said, 'Let's go for a walk, Leonard.'

'Where are you taking him?' asked Dad.

'Just to de shop,' said Mum. 'We can't keep him in all day. A little walk will do him good. It will do me good too.'

'Just be careful,' said Dad. 'An' don't talk too much.'

'Don't worry yourself,' Mum replied.

We went to the small corner shop not far away, but we walked the long way around, and we walked slow, which was OK with me because it was a warm day, and I did need some fresh air. It was hot, not as hot as in Maroon Town, but it was the best weather we had had for a while. It was a family-run shop that we had been to before when we wanted English things like cornflakes, beans, biscuits and spaghetti rings, because they didn't sell yam or anything like that. It was packed with so many goods sometimes we would knock things down accidentally, and sometimes the shopkeeper's children would serve customers. When we finished shopping we were waiting for an old lady in front of us to be served, but then a younger lady carrying a bag of sugar and a bag of flour came from behind us. As the old lady walked away, the younger lady put her sugar and flour on the counter and shouted at the shopkeeper.

'You're not going to serve the darkie before me, are you?'

The shopkeeper looked at my mother and me and then at the goods on the counter.

'She is next,' said the shopkeeper.

'I thought you looked out for your own, Margaret,' the younger woman said.

The shopkeeper smiled nervously.

'Of course, I care about my own! Now, do you need anything else?' the shopkeeper replied, and she served the lady.

'You were before that lady,' I said to Mum as we walked home. 'Why didn't you say something?'

'She was in a hurry,' she said awkwardly.

'But we were there before her! She didn't even ask you if she could go first, she just pushed in. And she called you a darkie.'

'This is their country, and I no want to cause any trouble. You could get into trouble if you answer them back,' she said.

'But you said we cannot give up.'

'I'm nar give up,' Mum replied forcefully. 'There is a time to reap, an' a time to sow. There is a time to speak, an' a time to stay silent.'

'Grandma said that lions always roar. Always,' I replied. 'An' we should be like lions. We should never be afraid to speak.'

'Forget about what your grandma said. She's not here.'

I wanted to shout, 'I will never forget what Grandma said,' but I didn't want to make Mum angry, so I bowed my head and said, 'But one day she might come here and she wouldn't want to know that people are being so rude to us.'

'She's not coming here, son.'

'Well, we might visit her, and what would we tell her about the way we live here?'

'Stop talking, Leonard.'

'But it's true,' I said.

She started getting louder. 'Stop talking.'

So I got louder. 'Grandma said—'

'Stop it, Leonard!' she shouted with such force that I had to stop. 'We're not going to see her again. Grandma's gone.'

I paused for a moment. 'Gone where?'

'Leonard. Your grandma dead.'

We both stopped walking. My whole body froze; I looked at my mum and for the first time in my life I had to give her a warning.

'You shouldn't say that. It's not nice. It can bring bad luck. Don't say it again.'

She looked directly at me. 'It's true, Leonard. Your grandma died a few weeks ago. We only just find out. It took two weeks for de letter to come from Jamaica. We won't see her any more. She gone.'

When I looked into Mum's eyes I could see she was telling the truth. She put her shopping bag on the floor and hugged me.

'We didn't tell you because with all that is happening

in Notting Hill an' other places, we just didn't want to upset you. You were beginning to settle down here so we wanted to wait until de time was right.'

I was angry, shocked, cold and hot at the same time. When I spoke, I was trying to stop myself from crying.

'When would be the right time to tell me?' I asked, my voice shaking.

'That's something we've been trying to work out, an' we just couldn't agree. Your dad will be angry with me now because I've told you.'

Then I couldn't stop myself. I cried, and cried, and cried. My face was wet, my shirt was wet, and when I tried to speak I had to take breaths in between the words.

'This country … has … taken everything … away … from me. My happiness … my friends. … and now, I'll never get to spend time with Grandma again. All for this stupid country.'

Mum guided me home. I don't remember seeing anything. I just couldn't stop thinking about Grandma and all the things she had said to me, all the things she had done for me, and all the love she had showed to me.

As soon as we walked into the room, Dad knew that Mum had told me. They started to argue, but I told them not to. I told them that if they argued I would run away and hate them for ever. I didn't mean it of course,

93

but I just wanted them to shut up.

How I really wished I could have seen Grandma one more time. Yes, I had my mum and dad, but in reality, it was my grandma who raised me. She was a Maroon, who had the Maroon spirit in her all her life. I had to get used to my life without her. I guessed this was part of growing up.

Chapter Sixteen

For the first few weeks of school, I couldn't stop thinking about my grandma. I could hardly concentrate in lessons – my mind kept drifting back to Jamaica, to our old home. I couldn't believe that Grandma wasn't still there, sitting on the step, or cooking in the kitchen, or chatting to people as they passed the house. My parents kept telling me that I had to start concentrating. It was an important year – I needed to prepare for secondary school, and I tried my best because I only had a year to catch up with all the other pupils. Having Mark as a friend helped me because I always had someone to talk to. But there were some children who would call me names. One day when I was playing football, I was running towards the goal with the ball, and a boy who didn't want me on his team shouted, 'Pass the ball to me, coconut.'

I ignored him, and scored. He looked angry because I didn't pass the ball to him, but I smiled knowing that

I put the ball in the net, and he didn't. Then Mark ran over to him and said, 'Don't call him names. Just because he's playing better than you. Just leave him alone.'

Most of the teachers were good but some of them would expect me to know everything about everything foreign. If they told me to do something they would end by saying things like, 'This is how we do it in this country.' But I never let it get to me. I would remember things Grandma said to me, and feel strong. I also began to realize that my mum and dad were really trying their best for me. They made sure I had everything that I needed, and they made sure that I felt loved.

Dad was working hard, and Mum began to look for a job. She went to as many shops, cafés and Post Offices as she could to ask if there were any vacancies. She had never worked in any of those types of places, but she was good at anything she did. Some of the people she worked for in Jamaica gave her letters to show any possible employers that she was a good, honest person. I could remember the posters on the streets of Jamaica asking people to come to England to work on the buses and the trains, and in the hospitals, but Mum said she just wanted a 'little' job, not too far from home, with a small company. But it turned out those jobs weren't so easy to get. Most places told her there were no vacancies and quickly hurried her out. Others stared at the letters from her old employers – they would make promises, but in the end they would reject her too. I felt so sorry for her, but she would just smile and say, 'What will be, will be.'

Soon autumn was over and the winter had arrived. I woke up on the first day of the Christmas holidays, hoping it had snowed like some of the boys in my class said it might, but the pavements were still grey and there were no icicles hanging outside my window. Over the holidays we watched a lot of television. On Christmas Eve, we watched *The Adventures of Tintin*, and on Christmas Day, after watching people sing carols, we listened to the Queen give a speech. I had never heard the Queen speak before – she sounded so serious. When I asked my dad why she was so serious he said, 'It's called the stiff upper lip, son. You never see the Queen and all the important people dancing and smiling like in the Caribbean. They always like to look strong, even when they're not.'

I had mixed up feelings about going back to school in January. I just wasn't really enjoying school. Most days when I came home, Mum would ask me what I had done that day, and most of the time I would tell her. But there were times when I wasn't quite honest. Like the time I was struggling with my work and Miss

Bright, the teacher that I liked the most of all, said, 'Don't worry. Your people are not very good when it comes to using your brains, but that's not a problem, because you're all so good at sport.'

I really wanted to answer back. I had seen other children answer teachers back, but we could never do that in Jamaica, and I didn't want to make trouble. The lion inside me wanted to roar, but I remembered that my mum said there were times to stay silent.

I also didn't tell my mum that one day when I was walking home from school a boy ran past me and slapped me round the back of my head shouting, 'Go back to Africa!' I didn't want to upset her with these things. In 1959, there wasn't so much fighting on the streets, but people were still writing to newspapers and appearing on television saying that black people are trouble makers, that we're dirty and that we should all go home. Mum and Dad talked about these things all the time. Dad said that sometimes people would say rude things to him on the bus. Sometimes, people even threw things at him! Knowing what my mum and dad were going through, I didn't want them to worry any more. My problems seemed small, compared to theirs.

But one Wednesday towards the end of the term I had had a really bad day. I was trying to be positive. I was trying to be good, but a stupid film called *Tarzan* had been on television the night before so all day kids were asking me silly questions again about where I came from, my hair, my skin colour. It really made me angry, but I kept calm. I walked to the school gate with Mark, who I thought by then had understood what I was going through, but he just made it worse.

'Actually,' he said. 'I've always wanted to ask you. Can you speak African?'

I really couldn't take any more.

'Move from me,' I said as I gritted my teeth. 'Just move. You're so stupid. I've never even been to Africa, but even I know there's so such language as African. How stupid can you get? Move from me.'

'OK, OK!' he said. 'But don't ask me to be your friend anymore. Don't ask me to stick up for you.'

'You never did anyway,' I hissed. 'Just move.'

As he walked away, I noticed a woman watching me from beside the school gate. She was wearing a bright green coat and had big blonde hair. I hadn't seen her around school but guessed she must be a new teacher or something.

'Don't worry, Leonard,' she said. 'You shouldn't take any notice of kids like that. They don't know anything. I blame the parents.'

'I'm OK, Miss. I try not to listen to them, but sometimes they just make me mad.'

'Well they make me mad too,' she replied.

'Are you going to report him to the head teacher, Miss?'

'Oh, I'm not a teacher,' she said, as if I should have known. 'I would if I was, but I'm not.'

'Well how do you know my name then?' I asked, puzzled. I was sure I'd never seen her before.

She looked down at her shoes. I think I'd made her uncomfortable, but I wasn't sure why. 'I have to go. You just take care now, and don't let anyone push you around.'

She hurried off and I turned and watched her walking down the street. I thought she might be meeting another pupil from school, or even a teacher, but she just kept going and didn't look back once.

As for Mark, well I saw him every day of the rest of the year, but I never spoke to him again. Not one word.

Chapter Seventeen

Over the summer holidays, Mum finally found a job, working in the local cinema. She had to collect tickets when people came in, and then she would serve ice cream in between the films. It was wonderful. She would take me to watch all the latest films, which I thought was great. Dad only took me around Manchester on his bus. Films took me around the world. I sat in the back row all day, watching film after film, like *Flash Gordon*, *The 7th Voyage of Sinbad*, *The Hound of the Baskervilles* and lots of cartoons.

After the summer holiday, not only was I going to a new school, a secondary school, but Mum had also found us a new place to live. There was much more space than our old place – it had two bedrooms, one of them mine, and a small bathroom and kitchen. I called it a bit of a house, but Dad said it was a flat. He'd got a pay rise at work and to celebrate he bought a new, bigger television.

We lived upstairs, and downstairs there was another family, Mr and Mrs Barry and their two children, Michael and Rosie. They owned a small shop not far from the house, where they sold baby clothes. They were always smartly dressed, but they weren't stuck up or anything, and were really welcoming when we moved in. Michael was thirteen. He had light hair and liked reading comics. Rosie was twelve. She had long dark hair and also liked reading, but she preferred books. She said she wanted to be a writer when she left school. I got on really well with Michael and Rosie; they were joyful, and funny, and because the garden was shared between the two flats, we played out there together most days. They never once asked me about the colour of my skin, or my hair, or the way the way I spoke. In fact, I was curious about the way they spoke. Once when I was playing with them in the garden Rosie and Michael started singing a song, and I told them that I really like the way they spoke, and the way they sang.

'That's because we're from Ireland,' said Rosie.

'Yes, Ireland,' said Michael. 'Can't you tell?'

'I don't know what Irish people sound like,' I said. 'I just thought you came from a different part of England.'

'No,' said Rosie. 'We come from a place called Killarney. The people were great there, but our parents wanted a different life for us because it's was hard for them there. So we came to England.'

'Wow,' I said surprised. 'That's a bit like us.'

'That's right,' said Rosie. 'You're not the only ones.'

My new school was called Anson Secondary School. Michael and Rosie were already there and we walked together every day. Although I was a small kid in a big school, I knew straight away that I was going to like it there. I found that I was good at mathematics, science and art. I did well in sports, and long-distance running became my specialty. This school didn't just have a playground. It had a sports hall, a running track, a football field and a big science block. Most of the pupils were white, but there were also some children from different parts of the world. Not many, but enough to stop me from feeling like the odd one out. Studying was taken more seriously here, so I studied hard and wasn't too concerned with making friends. But in the playground I talked, and played, with many kids, but most of all with Rosie and Michael.

I didn't find learning in school difficult; what I really found difficult was the British weather. It was really getting me down. It rained when it was cold, not just when it was hot. My mum had told me that some English people were nicer during the summer, and I had noticed that in the summer people smiled more, talked to each other more and were just happier. But the summer was so short. I still couldn't understand why my parents thought that life in England would be better for me than living in Jamaica. One winter's morning I woke up and I was feeling extremely cold and extremely miserable. I had seen Grandma in my dreams. We were in Jamaica, on the veranda, and she was talking to me about the old days. We were sitting beneath the bluest sky and watching the hummingbird that always visited the garden. But then I'd woken up and looked outside the window. The sky was grey. Grey because of the clouds, and grey because of all the smoke that was coming from the factories. I pulled myself out of my bed. My whole body felt heavy and slow. I had no energy. Mum and Dad were in the kitchen getting breakfast ready, as I slouched into the room and flopped into my seat.

'Good morning,' said Dad.

'Good morning,' said Mum.

'I don't know what's so great about this country.' I said. 'Are we ever going to go back to Jamaica?'

My dad turned to me and spoke firmly, but calmly. 'Of course not. This is where we live. This is home.'

'They don't even like us here,' I replied. 'And it's so cold.'

'Come with me,' Dad said, walking out of the kitchen and going into their bedroom. I followed him in. He motioned for me to sit down on their bed, then sat next to me.

'What's wrong?' he said.

'I don't like it here. I don't feel safe here. Me a try fit in but it just don't feel like home. Every day, me do what you tell me, me do what de teachers tell me, but at night when me close me eyes me see Jamaica. Me can't help it.'

'Let me tell you something, Leonard,' Dad said. 'The jobs are more secure here; the working conditions are safer. When you work here, you can keep the same job until you grow old! You would have a limited life in Jamaica. In Jamaica there is sunshine, there is space, there are wonderful animals, but I couldn't find work to feed you. I want you to have a better life than me, an' don't you want to see the world?' His eyes were wide open. He moved his hands everywhere as he spoke. 'When you grow old, you are still paid here – it's called a pension. In Jamaica only the people who work for the government can get a pension, and you're not going to work for de government.'

'I can work for the government. I can do what I like,' I said.

'Of course you can. But in Jamaica people like us

can't get jobs in government. You have to be light skinned. You have to be connected to the British. You have to have friends in high places.'

'That doesn't mean we shouldn't try,' I replied abruptly.

My dad raised his eyebrows and nodded his head in agreement with me. 'You're right, but my point is, there are no wars here. We don't have to wake up and worry about the country being taken over by a crazy army.

'Grandma said the country was taken over by a crazy army. The English,' I said.

'You're right. But that's the past. Look, in England if we are sick, we don't have to pay for a doctor. If we go to hospital, no one will ask us to pay the bill, and you don't have to pay to go to school. Count your blessings, son. It might be cold, but it is safe here.'

He stood up, walked to the window and called me over. 'Look out there.'

I got up and went to look out of the window. My dad pointed to an old man who was walking very slowly on the other side of the street.

'You see that man?' he continued. 'We are paying for each other's health care. He may not like us, but everybody contributes regardless, that's the kind of country that we live in.'

I stared at the frail old man. He was hunched over

a walking frame and wore a dishevelled raincoat. My dad wasn't finished.

'That man has paid into a pot for his entire life. He's funded your dentist, your school ... everything you take for granted, he helped to pay for it. When I go to work I help to pay for him.'

I thought it all sounded very nice, but I began to think about what it was like when I first went to school, and the way I was treated in the park, and the way some people treated my mum in shops and on the street.

'If this country is so good, why are there so many people who don't like us?' I asked.

He sat back down on the bed, and I sat next to him.

'You see, like your grandma told you, the British took over many countries. Many people all over the world, including people from Jamaica, had to fight for justice and freedom because of the way that people like us were being treated. We have been attacked, killed, starved and enslaved, but what you must remember is we must be better than the people who oppress us. We have to show them that we have dignity, and that we have pride in ourselves. The thing is, son, these people can't live in the past, and we shouldn't live in the past either. We are here now. We must make the most of it and move forward.'

So, though I had woken up feeling terrible, I went

to school feeling positive. I began to understand what people were talking about when they were talking about the welfare state. I realized how lucky I was. When I saw all the things we had in school, the sports equipment, the science equipment, and the books in the library, I told myself that I had to make the most of my time there, because so many kids around the world didn't have what we had. I reminded myself of these things often, so that every day I went to school was like a day towards a better future for me, and my mum and my dad.

Chapter Eighteen

After the talk that I had with my dad, I really did try to see the best in things. When the sky was grey, I tried to look between the clouds to see the sun. When someone was unkind to me at school, I ignored them and I went to have fun with Rosie and Michael instead. But things weren't perfect.

I was lying awake on my bed one night in February 1960, staring up at the ceiling and thinking about what I was going to do when I left school when I heard Mum scream from the other room. I jumped out of bed and ran to her, and found Dad sitting staring at the wall. Blood streamed from his nose and the side of his head.

'What happened?' I shouted. 'Dad, are you OK? Mum, what happened?'

My whole body trembled as I looked into my loving dad's swollen eyes. He was barely recognizable and he was struggling to breathe. Mum was rushing all over the room. She got a bowl, filled it with water, and placed it on the floor by Dad. She ran off and got a face cloth. I just didn't know what to do. I had never seen anyone bleeding so badly. My eyes went from Dad to Mum, and from Mum to Dad.

'What shall I do?' I asked.

'Nothing,' Dad said quietly.

'Can I help you, Mum?' As I spoke I could feel my heart pounding and hear my voice trembling.

'It's OK, Leonard,' Mum replied. 'I will take care of him.'

'I want to help.'

'Go back to bed, Leonard,' said Dad. 'I'm going to be OK.'

Mum started to wipe the blood from his face.

'Who did this to you?' my mum said. There was a tremble in her voice too, but my dad didn't answer.

'Dad,' I said. 'Please tell us. Who did this?'

'GO TO BED, LEONARD!' my dad shouted.

'NO!' I bellowed back. 'I have had enough of this place! I have had enough of seeing you both in pain! They can rebuild this land themselves. They do not even appreciate our help, and this is the thanks that you get?!'

'We should report this to de police,' Mum said. They cannot get away with this! Your son is right!'

'No. No police,' said Dad. 'They can't do anything.'

'You mean they won't do anything,' Mum said.

'They have to do something,' I said.

Mr Barry shouted up from the bottom of the stairs. 'You OK up there?'

'It's OK,' Mum called back. 'We're all right. I'll let you know if we need you.'

'Watch your dad,' Mum said to me as she walked towards the bathroom with the bowl.

I went to the chair where he sat breathing heavily and knelt down in front of him. He put his hand on the back of my head. Feeling helpless, I just held his knees until Mum came back. She had fresh water in the bowl and started to wipe his face with a cloth.

'Go to bed, Leonard,' said Mum. 'Your dad is going to be OK.'

'No,' I said.

'Go to bed, son,' Dad said. His nose had stopped bleeding, and he even managed to give me a small smile, though it looked like it hurt. 'Your mum's right – I'll be OK.'

I didn't want to leave him, but I did as I was told.

In bed I lay on my back with the lights off, but my eyes were open. I couldn't see anything. Only darkness. I could hear my parents talking next door; sometimes they were loud as if they were arguing, sometimes they were quiet, but I couldn't understand anything they were saying. Suddenly I heard footsteps coming towards my room and the door opened.

'Leonard,' Dad whispered. 'You still awake?'

'Yes, Dad,' I replied.

The light went on, and I sat up to look at him.

'What happened to you?' I asked. I spoke as quietly as I could. I didn't want him to shout at me, but I really wanted him to talk to me.

'Some bad people wanted to hurt me.'

'Why?'

'Because I'm a black man, son.' Dad sighed. 'Because I'm black.'

'Really? How do you know that's why they hurt you?'

'They told me, son. Every time they hit me, they told me.'

'Did you know them?' I asked.

'Of course not,' Dad said as he sat down on the bed. 'They are called Teddy Boys. They hate black people. They dress in big boots and they like to cause trouble. This is what they do.'

'If you know what they look like, and they always cause trouble, then we should call the poli—'

Dad raised his voice as he cut me off. 'If we tell the police, they won't do anything. They won't help us. I know other people who got beat up. They called the police, but nothing happened. So, it's not worth it.'

I could see that even speaking was hurting him, and the louder he spoke the more pain he seemed to be in. So I spoke softly. I just didn't want to agitate him any more.

'Grandma said, "We are freedom-fighting Maroons," but look at us now, we can't fight. Mum said, "We shall not be moved!" and "We cannot give up!" but then you said, don't call the police because they won't help us. I don't understand it, Dad. Who will defend us? Are we just supposed to take anything they do to us?'

Dad didn't reply. He just turned and left the room. I think he knew I had a point, and it was difficult for him to answer. In the next room I could hear him groaning as Mum treated his cuts and bruises. I lay on my back, looking at the ceiling, but now I was thinking that it was all my fault. My parents had come to England to give me a better life, but I had been bullied, my mum was made to feel she was not as good as white women, and now my dad was being beaten on the streets. This didn't feel like the safety that my dad told me about. This didn't feel like a better life. This was not how lions should live.

Chapter Nineteen

Dad spent Sunday doing nothing but trying to heal. He was adamant that he wasn't going to take time off from his job. He always boasted that he had never missed a day from work, and that he even went when he was feeling sick. Mum and I tried to convince him not to go, but he was determined, so I watched from the top of the stairs as he set off with a plaster on a shaved patch on his head where it had been cut, and a swollen lip. Mr Barry stopped him at the foot of the stairs.

'I'm OK,' I heard my dad say.

I watched him hobble out of the front door. I knew he had pride, and I knew that pride could never be taken by a group of Teddy Boys, whoever they were, but I was worried about him. If it had happened once it could happen again, but I was also proud of his strength and his bravery.

I really didn't want to go to school that day, but Mum insisted. I walked there with Michael and

Rosie and, in the end, I thought it was good that I went because the small things they talked about took my mind off things. I also thought that if Dad could pick himself up and go to work after what he'd been through, I should be able to go to school. But although I was trying to be strong and carry on, in class it was difficult to concentrate on lessons, and at break time I wasn't in the mood for playing games.

When I got home, Mum came down and let me in, but we were just halfway up the stairs when there was a knock on the door. Mum went back down and unlocked the door again. I could see a woman standing on the doorstep. Mum was in the way, but from the stairs I tried to look around her and I could see that the woman had very white skin, very red lips and very big blonde hair. She was also carrying a very big handbag. I looked carefully again, then I realized it was the same woman that spoke to me outside my old school on the day I fell out with Mark. Had she followed me home then? And why was she here now, two years later?

'Hello, love,' she said. 'Does Morris live here?'

'Who are you?' said Mum, folding her arms, her back stiffening

'I'm an old friend. A bus driver that I know told me that he got beaten up. I just wanted to see if he was all right. Is your son OK?' Her voice was a little bit wobbly as she shifted from one foot to the other. I could see her head bobbing over Mum's shoulder.

'What you a worry 'bout my husband for? And never mind my son,' Mum snapped back. She turned to me and shouted up the stairs. 'Go to your room.'

I did as I was told but I tried to listen to what they were talking about. I couldn't hear clearly, then after a little while my mum came back. She completely ignored me for most of the afternoon, but when I got the chance I asked her about what the blonde lady had wanted, and she just told me to mind my own business. She sounded angry, and because she sounded so angry I didn't want to tell her that I had met the lady before.

Mum prepared dinner as usual, and when Dad got home she tried to act as normal as possible. She asked him how he was feeling, and how it was at work. Dad wasn't looking well but at least he was walking upright. He took off his coat, went and took off his uniform, and then we all sat down to eat. Before we started Mum looked towards Dad.

'Morris. Pray.'

Dad looked back at Mum, then he looked at me.

'Leonard. You want to say a prayer?'

'No,' said Mum firmly. 'You pray, Morris.'

Dad bowed his head, and so did I, but then I opened my eyes and I saw my mother staring intensely at my dad's head as he prayed. His prayer was short and about being thankful for food, and ended with, 'Bless our family, we pray, this day. Amen.'

I started eating. Dad started eating. Mum just kept watching.

'So Morris,' she said. 'Who is Shirley?'

Dad was just about to put a piece of yam in his mouth. He paused, fork in hand, and thought for a moment.

'Shirley?' my dad replied as if he didn't know. 'Shirley who?'

'You tell me – and remember now, you have just prayed.'

Dad put his fork down on his plate. 'Let me think.'

'You shouldn't need to think,' Mum said. 'She knows you very well.'

'Oh, Shirley,' Dad said as if he suddenly remembered who she was.

'Oh, yes, Shirley, the woman you had when I was in Jamaica.' She turned to me. 'Leonard. Go to your room.'

'I'm still hungry,' I said.

'Take your food an' go to your room.'

She didn't shout, but I could tell by the tone of her voice that she wasn't going to take any backchat. I grabbed my plate of food and went to my room. Then

Mum got loud. I hadn't heard my mum sound this angry since my grandma threw her best dancing shoes out. This was a different kind of anger. My heart was beating so hard and fast I was surprised that my parents couldn't hear it through the walls.

'Shirley is me friend, Rita,' said Dad. 'She looked after me when I arrived.'

'Looked after you? Are you a child?'

'I was lonely! You were thousands of miles away from me. I had nobody to talk to.'

'So you choose a nice blonde woman. How come you didn't tell me?' Mum shouted.

'I didn't think you would understand. She is just a friend!'

'Just a friend. Just a friend. Do you really think I'm that stupid?' she said even louder.

They just kept arguing, and it was beginning to hurt my head. It got to a point when I just could take any more, so I ran back into their room.

'STOP IT!' I screamed, louder than either of them. 'JUST STOP IT. Stop shouting at each other.'

'Everything is OK, son,' said Dad.

'Everything is not OK, son,' said Mum.

'Go back to your room,' said Dad lowering his voice. 'We're just sorting through some grown-up business.'

'Yes, go, Leonard,' said Mum. 'I'll come an' talk to

you soon.'

After I went back to my room they carried on talking, but much quieter. I could feel that whatever they were saying they were trying to say without me hearing. About fifteen minutes later, Mum did come to talk to me, but when I asked her what was wrong, she just said, 'Don't worry. Me and your dad will sort it out.'

Chapter Twenty

When I woke the next morning, my dad was just finishing his breakfast in the kitchen. My mum didn't speak to me much until my dad had left. He stroked the back of my head and then walked out without a word. I felt uneasy. I didn't know exactly what, but he had done something that had really upset Mum.

'How much of our conversation did you hear last night, Leonard?' my mum asked as soon as he'd left.

'Not much of it,' I replied quickly.

'You know de lady that came to the house last night? Your dad apparently met her on a bus soon after he arrived here, and they became friends. He said she was the only English person who would speak to him when he first arrived. She showed him around Manchester and introduced him to people.'

'But I thought de other workers from Jamaica showed him around?' I said.

'Some did. But she took him to other places, places

he had only seen on the TV or from the bus window. She likes music and so they would go dancing.'

My mum choked on her last sentence but tried to reassure me. 'Your dad has said she tried to be his girlfriend, but he tried not to be her boyfriend.'

'What does that mean?' I asked.

'I have no idea, son. He said he saw her as company, but she wanted more. Him tell her him was married with a son, but she never thought we would come over. He said he wanted friendship, but she wanted domestic bliss. But that's not true.'

'It could be,' I said, trying not to sound like I was taking his side.

'No,' said Mum raising her voice. 'They went dancing in Liverpool. They stayed for the weekend. I'm a woman, an' I know that no man goes dancing with you, and stays with you for two nights if he only want to be your friend. Especially if she wants more. No way. I am no idiot.'

There was a long silence as I tried to think of what to say. I could see how emotional she was, and I didn't want to upset her any further.

'Do you think she's a bad person?' I asked. 'I don't think so. She was nice to me.'

As soon as I said that I realized what I had done. My mum responded quickly.

'What you mean she was nice to you? When was she nice to you?'

I hesitated, but I thought I had to be honest to her.

'She was outside Hyde School one day. She just said hello to me. It was the day me and Mark had an argument. When he was being stupid and asking me if I could speak African. I was really angry but she told me not to worry. She said I shouldn't take any notice of kids like that because they don't know anything. At first I thought she was a teacher.'

I could feel my mum thinking. She looked up to the ceiling and breathed deeply. Then she looked back at me.

'Did she say anything about your dad?'

I thought back to that day and ran through the conversation we'd had again. 'No.'

'Are you sure?'

'Yes!' I said.

'Leonard. You wouldn't lie to me, now, would you?'

'No, I'm telling the truth! She just told me to take no notice of people that were rude to me. I thought she was a teacher.'

'And she didn't mention me?'

'No.'

I stared at my mum. 'Will you forgive him?'

She paused, kissed her teeth, and poured boiled

water from the kettle into the cup over the tea bag. Then she kissed her teeth again.

'I don't know. As far as I'm concerned he done a bad, bad thing. How do I know he won't see her again? How do I know he's not seeing her now?'

With that statement, she looked me straight in the eye and continued to speak. 'When you are older, Leonard, and you meet a woman, you must treat her like she is your queen or you will lose her. Women are made to feel like they belong to men. We don't have to belong to men, but if you are to make a woman truly happy, you must respect her as an individual, and always stay faithful to her. Love is not just about saying the right words or buying the right things. It's about being honest with each other. It's about trust.'

'Yes, Mum.' I replied.

'Good. Never forget that, you hear. Never forget that. Now hurry up and go to school.'

Chapter Twenty-one

I was told off a few times by teachers that day for not paying attention, but the problem was I had so many other things on my mind. I couldn't act as if everything was fine. I couldn't forget how my dad got beaten up, and how my dad made my mum feel. I couldn't get the blonde woman off my mind. Mathematics, English, Geography, all seemed so unimportant when we had so many problems at home. At break times in the playground I couldn't talk to anyone. Rosie and Michael tried talking to me, but they soon got the message that I needed to be alone. I just found a corner and passed time there.

When I arrived home the door was locked, and though I knocked for a good five minutes nobody came to let me in. Finally, Mr Barry opened it.

'Sorry, Leonard,' he said. 'I was in the garden and I only just heard you knocking. Your mother has gone out, but she asked if you could wait in our flat until your father came home. I said yes, of course, so come on in.'

He gave me a strange look, like he felt sorry for me, though I wasn't sure why. *Perhaps he heard Mum and Dad shouting last night*, I thought. Michael and Rosie came back a few minutes later, but their dad quickly shooed them into the other room, saying they had homework to be getting on with, and leaving me alone with my thoughts. Time passed slowly, and I took out a book from my school bag and started to read.

'Psst, Leonard,' Rosie said as she stuck her head round the door. 'Everything all right? Why didn't you walk home with us? Where's your ma?'

I shrugged; I couldn't think where she might have gone. She never worked hours that stopped her from taking care of me, and if she was going somewhere, she always told me where. All I could do was worry, but then I heard the front door open and close, and footsteps going upstairs.

'Mr Barry?' I shouted. 'I just heard Mum come home, so I'm going back upstairs now!'

'OK' he called back from the kitchen. 'Just take care and let me know if you need me.'

I opened the door, ready to tell Mum off for making me sit awkwardly in the Barrys' flat for hours. But it wasn't my mum taking her shoes off in the corridor, it was my dad. He was looking a bit better than when he left, but I didn't expect him to smile.

'You've been downstairs with the Barrys. How are they?'

'I only saw them for a short time, but they're OK.'

I started to follow him up the stairs. He turned the handle of the flat door to find it was locked, so he found the key for that lock and as he was opening the door, he chuckled and said, 'So your mum is locking you out now. Have you been causing trouble?'

He walked into the room, with me right behind him, 'Rita?' he called.

'She's not here,' I said impatiently. 'That's why I was waiting downstairs.'

'Let's see if she leave some food for us,' Dad said walking into the kitchen. But soon he walked back.

'Well, there's a pot of food, but it cold,' he said. 'Maybe she gone shopping.'

He stood in the centre of the room looking around, then he walked over and looked in the wardrobe. He bent down and looked under the bed. Suddenly he started to move very quickly. He looked at the coat hooks. He went into my room. Then came out and exclaimed, 'She's gone. She's gone, Leonard. She's left us.'

I said nothing aloud, but in my mind I said, 'She's

left you, not us. You did this.'

My dad sat on his bed with his head bowed, just staring at the floor. I stood just looking at him. As I looked at him I felt no sympathy for him at all. My mind went back to two days before, and how sorry I felt for him when those Teddy Boys beat him up. He couldn't help that. But this was brought on himself. After speaking to Mum I knew how she was feeling so I just had nothing to say to him. He was watching me, but I shook my head at him and went into my bedroom.

After ten minutes of silence, I began to hear Dad moving around. Then he came into my room. He looked like a broken man. He could barely look me in the eyes.

'Son. Please just make yourself something to eat and then just stay inside, right? Don't go anywhere outside. I have to go out.'

I wanted to know what he was thinking. I wanted to know where he was going. But I just nodded my head, then he turned and left.

Chapter Twenty-two

Mum had left a pot of black-eyed peas soup, the kind that was full of yam and potatoes and other vegetables, so it was a meal in a pot. I heated it up and went into my parents' room to eat and watch television. As I sat down I noticed a piece of paper on the bed. I picked it up and read it.

Morris,

All those years I was in Jamaica I dedicated my time to looking after our son and your mother. Your family is the only family I had, now our family is the only family I have. Not once did I look at another man. Not once did I cheat on you. You hurt me bad, Morris, so I'm gone. Don't come looking for me. I will come back for my son when I'm ready, so you can go dancing with your lady friend. You can spend as many weekends in Liverpool with her as you like. I'm gone.

Goodbye.

My mum had gone, but I wished she had taken me with her. I didn't really want to be alone with my dad, and suddenly I didn't feel like eating, but I ate as much as I could and then I went to bed. As much as I tried, I couldn't sleep. I just lay there worrying about my mum and being angry with my dad. Finally, at 1 a.m., I heard him come home. He pushed open my door and peered in at me.

'Where's Mum?' I asked him in the darkness.

'I don't know.' My dad sounded tired. 'I went to the cinema and they said she asked for some time off. I went to her hairdressers and they haven't seen her. I walked the streets looking for her but I can't find her.'

'I read the note she left,' I said.

He turned the light on. 'This is big-people business. You shouldn't get yourself involved in big people's things.'

'I'm already involved. Your friend came to my school and spoke to me.'

I could see the surprise on my dad's face. The surprise was followed by anger. 'I told her to leave me and my family alone.'

'So, why won't she?'

Dad paused for a moment. 'I don't know. She says she still wants to be my friend. She wants to be friends with your mum and you, as well. But I told her that

129

can't work. What did she say to you?'

'Nothing much. She just said I mustn't let anyone push me around.'

He stepped into the room and sat on my bed. Anger flared inside me – I didn't want him in my room; I didn't want him anywhere near me. As soon as he went to speak, I interrupted him.

'How we going to find her?' I demanded.

'I don't know, but we will.'

'This is all your fault, Dad.'

'I know, and I'm sorry. But I will find her and we will work it out.'

'I read the note. She said don't go looking for her.'

'But I have to, son.'

He stood up and continued talking. 'I went to the phone box and phoned the bus company when I was outside. I told them I need to have a day off tomorrow. They said OK. You get some sleep.'

I tried again, but I just couldn't. I would doze off and wake up. Doze and wake up. Every time I woke up, I would listen for Mum. I couldn't imagine her out on her own. I thought she might come back in the middle of the night, but when I heard Dad moving around in the morning and not speaking, I knew she had not returned home.

I could see this was really affecting Dad. He spoke

very little. He kept gazing around the room as if he was still searching for clues. His eyes were red. He looked as if he had been crying, but I still found it hard to feel sorry for him. He didn't even bother making breakfast. He just heated the soup that was leftover and offered some to me.

'No, thanks,' I said, and poured some cold milk over some cereal. As we both stood in the kitchen eating he told me to hurry up and get ready for school.

'I'm not going to school,' I told him.

'You have to,' he replied.

I set down my spoon. 'I'm not going and you can't force me.'

My dad put down his bowl of soup and glared at me. 'How dare you speak like that!' he said. 'I am your dad and you must listen to me.'

'There is no way I can go to school an' study – I'm worried about you, I'm worried about mum, and I'm worried about our future. If you send me to school I won't go. I'll just run away an' that will be two of us you'll be looking for. I'm not going to school. I can't do it.'

He looked at me intensely for a while. He just knew I was serious.

'Fine,' he said finally. 'I have to go out, but if you're not feeling well you can stay at home.'

'Where are you going?' I asked.

'To look for your mum.'

'Well, I'm going with you.'

'You can't,' he said.

'Why not?'

'Because this is big-people business.'

'Stop saying "this is big-people business". If it's your business, and it's mum's business, then it's my business too.'

Chapter Twenty-three

We spent the whole day walking around the streets of Manchester looking for Mum. We went back to the cinema, the hairdressers and the Caribbean Community Centre. Dad started asking any random Jamaicans he saw whether they had spotted someone matching her description. We also took some short rides on buses using his pass, but we really were getting nowhere. Dad just didn't have a clue where to look, and I could see him getting more desperate as the day went on. Early in the evening, he gave up.

For dinner, he was going to heat up even more of the soup Mum had cooked, but I wasn't having any of that. I helped him cooked some white rice and stewed cabbage. After we had eaten I went into my room and got the postcard that Dad had sent me when I was small in Jamaica. It made me think of the times when my dad was my hero. I then went into my parents' room, sat down, and had another look at the note that Mum had left. A few lines stuck with me.

Your family is the only family I had, now our family is the only family I have.

I knew that my mum didn't know her parents, but I didn't know why. I wasn't in the mood for speaking to my dad, but there were questions I needed to ask.

'Why doesn't Mum know her parents?'

'It was too difficult to explain to you when you were young, but she has no idea who her parents are.'

'Doesn't she know anyone from her family?' I asked.

'No. Because she doesn't know who her parents are, she has no way of tracing other relatives.'

I had always thought that I might have relatives on my mum's side, and the only reason I never met any of them was because they were all from another part of Jamaica.

'So, when you met Mum she was living on the streets?'

'No,' Dad replied quickly. 'She didn't ever live on the street; she grew up in an orphanage. She was only told that someone left her there. She doesn't know if that was her mum, or someone who found her. But when I met her she was living in a hostel. By then she could take care of herself.'

Living in an orphanage and in a hostel would have been better than living on the streets I thought, but it still must have been a very hard life. I looked at my dad and I could see that he was having difficulty talking about it. Then his face muscles relaxed, and there was a hint of a smile at his lips.

'When I met her I didn't care where she came from. She was just beautiful. We were always making each other laugh. We spent every moment we could with each other, and we looked out for each other. When me an' her walk down the street all de man them jealous, because they know that I have a good woman.'

He was smiling properly now, but I had to burst his bubble.

'If she was such a good woman, why did you hurt her so badly? And don't tell me it's big-people business.'

He looked at me and he could see I was serious. We glared at each other, but I wasn't going to blink first. He did. Then he looked down at the floor and started speaking.

'When you're young you can have lots of plans. Some of them will work out, others won't. Sometimes you get to where you want be but not de way you expected.'

He looked up, reached over and took the postcard from my hand. He stared at it for a while and began to speak again.

'I can remember de moment I stepped on this ship.

The *Empire Windrush*. We all had plans, some might say dreams. Yes, you could say that ship was packed with dreams. Whatever you want to call them, all I know is that I wanted to make a better life for you, an' help England. I used to call myself a Windrush man. We were de Windrush generation, an' you are a child of that generation, just like I wrote on this card.'

He glanced around the room, at the life he had made here, breathing deeply and biting his lip. For the first time ever, I thought I might see my dad cry. But he didn't. He looked down again and continued to speak.

'When I stepped off this ship, I knew no one in this country. All I had was de address of a hostel that would give me a place to stay free for one month, an' some addresses of companies that were looking for workers. In them days, the British were so desperate for help to build de country back up after de war, that I went for three interviews an' got three jobs. One for de General Post Office, one for a chemical factory, an' one driving buses. I knew nothing 'bout chemicals, an' I didn't fancy walking de street delivering letters, but I could drive an' I wanted to get to know de city. That's what it was like when I first come here. Plenty of work. Then just a few years later people started saying that we were taking their jobs.' He sighed. 'Anyway, I find a room to live in, and I start driving buses. I only knew

136

a couple of Jamaican men, so when I met Shirley on my bus an' we got on well, I was just pleased to have made a friend. She showed me around the city, made me feel welcome.'

He stopped talking and hesitated. I was convinced that he wasn't sure if he should say any more. He looked up, looked down, and continued. 'First we used to go around Manchester, then we went to Wigan, Bolton and Leeds. We were just sightseeing. Then we started to go dancing, and then we went to Liverpool. I was very bored, and I very lonely. All I used to do was work, so she was company. That's all.'

'That's not all,' I said, anger fizzing through me. 'I'm not stupid. If that was all why didn't you tell Mum? Why did you hide it?'

'All right, Leonard. All right. I know I done bad. Me know – and me really regret it. Me mek a big mistake, but me never say anything because me know your mother wouldn't understand.'

'That's de problem,' I said fuming. 'She would understand. Even I understand. You were wrong. It's as simple as that. You were wrong.'

'Yes. I was wrong,' he said. 'I'm really sorry. Please forgive me. You must forgive me.'

'Don't worry about me forgiving you. You need Mum to forgive you. If she does, I might.'

I passed him the note and reminded him of what it said.

Don't come looking for me.

'I don't think we should keep looking for her. I think she wants to be alone,' I said.

'I think you're right,' he said.

Chapter Twenty-four

We stopped looking for Mum, which meant I had to spend more time with Dad. I really didn't want to be around him, but I had no choice. Going to school was a way of getting away from him, and when I was at home we didn't talk much. He knew that I thought that he had let me, as well as Mum, down. Then one night as I was staring at the same bit of ceiling that I was spending so much time looking at, it came to me. I knew exactly where Mum was. The next morning, as soon as my dad was gone, I changed out of my school uniform and set off to find her. I didn't tell Michael or Rosie why I wasn't going to school. I didn't even know the address of where I was going, I just knew my way from where we used to live. After walking for about forty-five minutes to our old house, then walking for about another ten minutes to my final destination, I knocked on the front door, and it was opened by Aunt Maud. She looked very surprised to see me.

'Leonard! What are you doing here?'

I got straight to the point. 'I want to see my mum.'

'What makes you think she's here?' Aunt Maud asked, her hands on her hips.

'I just know,' I replied.

She looked at me very carefully. Then she looked up and down the road.

'Where's your dad?'

'At work,' I replied.

'Did you tell him you were coming here?'

'No. He thinks I'm at school.'

'OK,' she said. 'Come in.'

I stepped into the hallway of the house and Aunt Maud guided me to a room on the left and, standing right there, was my mum. I hugged her as hard as I could, and she squeezed me back. She held my hand and led me to the settee. When we sat down the first thing she said was, 'Are you sure your dad never follow you here?'

'I'm sure,' I replied. 'He's at work, but I figured out you'd be here.'

'So how are you?' she said tenderly.

'Me all right.'

'Are you eating?' She patted my stomach.

'Yes, Mum.'

'It doesn't look like it. So tell me. What is your dad

saying?' She turned and looked away as she spoke.

'The day after you left, we spend de whole day looking for you. I read de note you left for him, so I reminded him that in your note you said not to go looking for you. Since then he's been going to work, an' I went back to school. But he knows that I'm angry with him too. I've hardly spoken to him.'

'Really?' Mum said, surprised.

'He keeps saying what happens between you and him is big-people business, but I know what he's done, and him know sey me angry.'

'Good,' said Mum. 'He should know.'

Aunt Maud left the room, but I could hear her moving around the house. It felt good to be with Mum again. I felt like I didn't want to leave her side. Although I wasn't at home, I felt at home, because I was with Mum.

'That man really hurt me, you know, son?' she said.

'Me too.'

'I've been so good to that man, an' look how him treat me.' Her voice was strained.

'I know, Mum,' I said sympathetically. 'I know you don't have contact with your family, but Dad tell me you don't even know them.'

'That's why I'm so hurt. I didn't grow up in a family, so when I started a family, I wanted it to be a tight, honest family. He let me down badly.'

Mum stood up. 'I'll be back in a moment.'

When she returned she was carrying a tray with orange squash and a packet of digestive biscuits on it. I could still hear Aunt Maud in the hallway, and then she joined us. Mum put the tray down on the table and told me to eat and drink, and I did. I almost drank the whole bottle and ate the whole packet. I didn't realize how hungry I was, but Mum must have known.

'You need some good food,' she said. 'And you need to go home.'

'When do you think you'll be coming home?' I asked, almost afraid to hear the answer, in case she told me she was never coming back.

'Now,' she said. 'I'm taking you home now.'

I jumped up off the seat.

'Really?'

'Really,' she replied.

'Are you going to stay?'

'Well, that depends on your dad,' she said. 'I don't want leave you; I want us to stay together, but I want to punish him. I want him to understand what him do.'

'I understand.'

'And I wanted him to suffer,' she said.

'He's suffering for sure,' I said.

'Good,' said Mum. She smiled. 'Let's go.'

142

I was so happy, and I could see that Aunt Maud was happy for us both.

When we left the room, Mum's suitcase was in the hallway. Aunt Maud had placed it there, ready for our departure. I remembered watching Mum struggle with the suitcase when she and I were coming to England. I was too young, and too small to help her. But I wasn't now. I picked up the suitcase and followed Mum and Aunt Maud outside. Aunt Maud went to the house next door. She had also arranged for her Jamaican neighbour to take us back home. His car had big leather seats that smelt old. We had to take children's toys that were scattered all over the seats and put them on the back shelf. Aunt Maud sat in the front and me and Mum sat in the back. We didn't say much. Aunt Maud asked him a few questions about how his family were getting on, but that was all. I could sense that she didn't want to say too much in front of him. When we arrived at the house the neighbour waited while Aunt Maud followed us upstairs, where she quickly said goodbye and left. Mum and I were truly alone at last.

Mum didn't put her suitcase away. She placed it carefully by the door, and then she made me some ackee and saltfish. We sat and ate together. I kept glancing up, just to check she was still there and hadn't disappeared again.

'I'm happy to be home,' Mum said as we finished our meal. 'I'm happy to be with you. But if he doesn't show me that he really regrets his actions, an' he'll never do it again, I won't stay.'

'Nor would I,' I said.

Chapter Twenty-five

When Dad walked in the door the first thing he saw was the suitcase, then he saw Mum. He didn't say a word. Mum looked at him without saying a word, and then I left the house, without saying a word. I didn't want to be around while they were talking, and I thought they wouldn't want me around. I walked aimlessly for over an hour, and when I felt I had walked enough for that day I returned home. As I walked up to the door the ground–floor curtain twitched and I saw Mr Barry signalling me to wait. I didn't have a key anyway, so I thought he was simply letting me in, but when he opened the door he told me to come into his flat. Michael, Rosie and Mrs Barry were in the front room.

'Your parents have been doing a lot of shouting,' said Mr Barry. 'It's not as bad as it was fifteen minutes ago, but I think you should just wait here for a while.'

As I looked around, I realized that none of them were doing anything. They had been listening to all the arguing upstairs. I was embarrassed.

'I'm sorry,' I said.

'Don't be sorry,' said Mrs Barry. 'It's called life.'

While I was there I didn't hear much arguing, apart from slightly raised voices, and they got quieter and quieter. After ten minutes, Mr Barry said 'I think it's OK now. Why don't you go up, Leonard, but if you need to get away, you're welcome to come down here.'

When I entered our flat the first thing I noticed was the suitcase. It was gone. Mum's coat was hanging on the back of the door, and Dad was sitting at the table eating fried plantains with beans. Mum smiled at me.

'Get your things ready for school tomorrow,' she said, and I knew everything was all right again. Well, as all right as could be. Mum said no more. Dad said no more. I asked no questions. I knew what Mum wanted from Dad, so I presumed that she got it.

I was proud of my mum, and slowly I began to build back my relationship with my dad. Over the next year, we went to the park now and then to play football, but Dad was definitely slowing down. I could easily outpace him, and soon, I grew taller than him too. After everything came out about Shirley, he treated me with a bit more respect. I didn't get bossed around so much; instead, I got asked my opinion on things. If I was having a problem at school with students, teachers or work, I could talk to him about it.

Mum was getting to know many more people and had her own circle of friends. Sometimes I would come home from school to find a group of women in the flat talking and laughing. Sometimes I would be the butt of their jokes. Like the time I came home to find a flat full of women, and one of them said, 'Leonard, how was school today?'

'Fine,' I replied.

'How was the school meal?'

'Fine,' I said.

'How was the walk home?'

'Fine,' I said.

'How was your girlfriend?'

'Fine,' I said. 'No. Not fine. I don't have a girlfriend.'

The women were falling over themselves laughing. The one asked, 'Are you sure you nu have a girlfriend?'

'I'm sure,' I replied.

'OK,' she said. 'You want me fix you up with my daughter? She could do with a nice boy like you to take her to de cinema.'

'I have no time for cinema now. Me have to concentrate on my schoolwork.'

The big news in the Jamaican community was that

after years of fighting for independence, and years of politicians talking about independence, it was going to happen. Jamaicans were desperate for independence. They were angry that so much of the wealth that they were creating wasn't being spent at home, and they wanted an education system that made them proud of themselves, and not just subjects of the British Empire. So, on Sunday 5 August 1962, during the school summer holiday, at around seven o'clock, we walked to the Caribbean Community Centre. We had not eaten at home because we knew there was going to be lots of food waiting for us, and when we got there, there was. There were rows of tables full of food and drink, and there was a big sound system playing Jamaican Ska music very loudly. The food was supposed to last through the night, because the next day Jamaica was going to get its independence. I had seen Jamaicans in the streets, in the shops. I had even been to the Caribbean Community Centre and met Jamaicans there before, but this was the largest number of Jamaicans I had seen in one place since leaving Jamaica, and they were also the happiest.

There were speeches, and a talent show with men, women and children singing traditional Jamaican songs. The air was filled with a mixture of the strong smell of curried goat, and cigarette smoke. I was amused to see my mum and dad dancing together for the first time.

After all the ups and downs we had gone through, from the time Dad had left Jamaica till Jamaican independence, it was a good to see them relaxing. I too was happy. A girl that I had never seen before came up to me and gave me a Jamaican flag. This was the new flag with no British symbols on it. With the black, yellow, and green flag in my hand, I started to wave it about. I danced with everyone that walked past me. We all danced until the music stopped. Then there was a loud countdown to midnight. Everyone really went crazy shouting about how free Jamaica would be, and of the wonderful future to come. In Manchester we were six hours ahead of Jamaica, so when we were celebrating, they were still waiting. We left at one o'clock in the morning; we weren't going to wait for another six hours to celebrate again, but some were.

As we were walking home I asked my parents what independence really meant.

Mum said, 'Right now, independence means Jamaicans can organize their own dances, fly their own flag, an' sing their own national anthem.'

She just didn't sound serious, so I enquired more.

'Is that all?'

'No,' said Dad. 'There is more to it than that. This is not de independence your granddad died for. We believe in real independence. An independent country is a country that controls its own destiny. It has its own police, its own laws, and its own court.'

'That makes sense to me,' I said.

'That makes sense to me too,' said Dad. 'What doesn't make sense is de location of Jamaica's highest court.'

'Where is it?' I asked.

'London,' he replied.

Chapter Twenty-six

As soon as I was able to, at the age of sixteen, I left school and found a job. At first I used to walk into factories and shops and ask if they had any work. I had no qualifications, but people kept saying there were plenty of jobs around and I would get one soon. One day, Dad came home and gave me a piece of paper with a man's name on it, and an address. The man was called Fred. His brother drove buses with Dad and he was looking for an apprentice. I went to see him the next day, and the day after that I started working for him. He was around my dad's age, cheerful and talkative. When he saw me on my first day in my new overalls, he looked me up and down and smiled.

'It's a long time since I've seen overalls so clean. Clean overalls usually mean you're not working, but it's your first day so you're OK.'

Then he opened a tin of magnolia paint, gave me a paint brush, pointed to a wall, and said, 'Paint it.'

'Just like that?' I asked.

'Yes. Just like that,' he replied.

I got a small step ladder, went to the top right-hand corner, and started painting. Fred stood behind and started talking.

'Right. You're now an apprentice painter and decorator. I don't expect you to know everything, but you'll learn everything if you listen to me. Now, make your brush strokes more even, and don't rush it.'

I adjusted my hand on the brush and changed the action of my strokes to make them smoother, and I slowed down.

'That's better,' he said. 'You've got it already. We're going to be hanging wallpaper tomorrow, so just do as I say and you'll be fine. Your overalls won't be so clean, but you'll be fine.'

My parents still sounded very Jamaican, but they kept telling me that I sounded as if I was born in Manchester, and I was beginning to believe them, because people stopped asking me about my accent. Fred was born in Manchester, so I think after listening to him every day I was beginning to sound like him.

We moved into our own small house that we rented from the council. Mum decided to train as a nurse and Aunt Maud helped her put together an application. She soon began working in our local hospital as a state registered nurse, or SRN, and her face was full of pride as she placed her badge on her uniform each morning.

Meanwhile, my dad continued to work as a bus driver. Even though he'd always said he loved his job, I was now old enough to understand that every day people would say racist things to him. Sometimes, when I rode on the bus with him, I would have to grip the seats to contain my rage when I heard someone call him a name, or mutter something under their breath. Sometimes, the bus conductor was white, and sometimes black. Some of the white conductors would defend Dad when people said bad things to him, but some didn't. One day when there was a black conductor on the bus, a white passenger refused to pay. Dad and the conductor told the passenger that they had to pay or they would be breaking the law.

'This is my country and I don't have to pay a blackie for anything,' the passenger shouted, getting right up close in my dad's face. 'I don't know what this place is coming to! Why should I have to give money to you lot? You're in our country now – we tell you what to do; you don't tell us.'

Despite times like these, my dad insisted that he enjoyed his job.

'I get to meet the good people of England, as well as the bad, and the good people always outnumber the bad,' he told me with a shrug.

'Teenagers shouldn't just sit at home with them parents,' said Mum. 'They should start living their own life.'

Dad agreed, adding, 'But you got to be careful out there.'

I stayed friends with Rosie and Michael, although I didn't see them much, but I started going out and meeting new friends. My favourite place was a club called Rocket. I came across it one night when I was walking around, looking for somewhere to go; it looked friendly so I paid three pounds and went in. As soon as I went in, a well-dressed man came up and spoke to me.

'Are you new here?'

'Yes,' I replied. 'How do you know?'

'I can tell by the way you're looking around,' he said. 'And I come here all the time, so I know most people. Relax, have a good time. It's great here,' he said. Then he walked away.

Soon after, someone else came up and asked me similar questions. That happened all the time, and soon I got to know people's names. I went there a few times and I soon found out that what Dad said was true. A lot of the people I was meeting were white, and most of them were good.

I was beginning not to care who was black or white;

154

it was all about meeting good people. Actually, we didn't say good people – we said cool people. Ska music became very popular and I started going to clubs. When I first started going most of the other people were Jamaican, then people from other Caribbean islands would come, and then I was amazed to see that many white people were dancing with us in these clubs, and they were loving the music.

These people are cool, I thought. I need to dance with these people. And I did.

One night in a club called The Moss, I met my first girlfriend. I was dancing and she came straight up to me and said, 'It's no fun dancing on your own, you know. Do you want to dance with me?'

I wasn't sure if I heard correctly, and the music was loud. So just to make sure I shouted, 'What?'

'Do you want to dance?' she shouted back.

'I think so,' I said shyly.

'Well, you either do or you don't. Which one is it?'

'Yes, please,' I said, and we danced.

'I have a job, you know,' I said, as the music came to an end. I felt like I needed to impress her. 'Do you want a drink?'

'I didn't want to dance with you because you have a job,' she said smiling. 'I want to dance with you because I think you're nice. You dance nice; you look nice ... you're just nice. But if you're buying a drink, I'll have one.'

Anna was born in Manchester and had never left the city. She had long black hair that went down to her waist and green eyes. I had never seen green eyes like hers. She told me that although she had never left Manchester, when she danced to reggae music, she felt like she was in Jamaica. It didn't do that for me, but I could understand what she meant.

'You've got reggae in your soul,' I said as we headed back to the dance floor. 'You dance good.'

'Thank you,' she said, wrapping her arm around my neck.

Anna and I continued to meet up with each other for the next eighteen months; we would go to reggae clubs and she started to bring her friends and I brought mine. Soon there was a small group of us that would go dancing all over Manchester. I started to feel like I belonged in England. It didn't matter to Anna or me or any of our friends what colour you were – our group were white, Asian, black. We didn't sit down and say we wanted a multi-coloured gang; we just liked music and dancing, and that was all that mattered. But sometimes we were reminded of the real world. Sometimes people would look at us strangely, sometimes they would say things to us, but when we were in the group it didn't matter. We had each other.

One night, me and Anna said goodbye to our friends after a night of dancing, and set off for home. But as we were walking across a small green, a place we had walked through loads of times before, we noticed a group of white men following us. They were around the same age as me, and I could just tell they were looking for trouble. My heart sank as I remembered what happened to my dad many years before.

'Look, lads!' the plump, red-faced leader said.

'It's the black and white minstrel show,' his friend said laughing. My heart sank as I recognized the man's face. It was Mark from Hyde Primary School. He had changed. He was much taller, his hair was cut really short, and when he spoke I could see hatred on his face.

'Is there a problem, boys?' I replied, pulling Anna closer.

'What do you think?' Mark said, with a sinister grin on his face.

'Hello, Mark,' I said, hoping that if he recognized me, the situation might calm down. 'How are you?'

The group all looked at Mark.

'Do you know this wog?' one of them asked.

'No,' said Mark staring straight into my eyes. 'I've never seen this wog before in my life. Have I, wog?'

The way he kept using that word really angered me,

but we were outnumbered, so I played along with him.

'No,' I said. 'I've never seen you before. I heard one of your friends call you Mark.'

He came and stood right in front of me, putting his nose right against mine. 'Right. Now what I want you to do for me and my friends is speak African.'

'There's no such language as African,' I said.

'Don't answer me back, wog. Just give us some of that African lingo.'

'Didn't you hear what he said?' Anna asked, trying to move between us. 'There's no such language as African.'

'Don't you speak, traitor,' said Mark. 'You should know better.'

Trying to move his attention away from Anna, I started to tell him, 'I'm from Jamaica and Jamaicans speak Eng—'

But before I could finish the sentence, he hit me with a right hook to my jaw. I lost all feeling in my legs, so I fell down to the ground. I was on my hands and knees. My head was fuzzy. It was hard to think, but I remembered Anna, and I didn't want them to start beating her. I knew I couldn't fight all of them, but felt I had to protect her, even if I could just wrap myself around her. So I tried to stand up again, but as soon as I started, the five of them circled and kicked at my

158

body and face. I couldn't see, but it felt as if they were all wearing heavy boots. I could hear Anna screaming, but I couldn't help her, then I took a powerful kick to the side of my head and I blacked out.

As I awoke in the hospital bed, my mum's blurry face loomed above me. I struggled to focus – my eyelid was split, and my face was covered in stitches. I was in a private room. I tried to sit up, but my mum pushed me back down on the bed, her face full of love, worry and sympathy.

'Shhh,' she said, stroking my head. 'You just lie down there.'

'Where's Dad?' I asked. It was hard to speak. I felt as if my chest had caved in.

'Your dad had to go away on business. Don't worry about that now.'

My mum's eyes were filling with tears. I could see she was struggling to hold those tears back, and her eyes were bloodshot.

'He's a bus driver,' I said with great difficulty. 'What kind of business could he possibly be on?'

I didn't understand why he wouldn't have come with Mum. Surely he'd want to be here to look after her and to make sure I was OK. A soft cough came from the corner of the room and I looked up to see Anna waiting there. She came over and put a hand on my chest. 'I have to go now,' she said. 'I just wanted to make sure you're all right.'

'Are you OK?' I asked. 'I don't really remember what happened.'

'I'm fine,' she said. 'I got pushed to the floor, and when I stood up to try and help you, they pushed me to the floor again. When I managed to get up, I ran as quickly as I could to the phone box and called the ambulance.' She paused and looked over to Mum. 'I have to go now. Please take care. You have a lot to deal with, but you know I'm here if you need me.'

After Anna left, it was just me and Mum, but she wasn't saying anything, just looking deep into me. I didn't have the energy to shout, so I just tried to speak and forcefully as I could.

'Where is Dad?' I asked. 'I know you're not telling me something.'

But Mum just repeated that he was away on business, like a record stuck replaying one track over and over again. But I knew that if my dad had travelled thousands of miles to build a new life for us, there was no way that he would prioritize any kind of business over being by my side when I needed him. I tried to sit up in the bed again, but Mum rushed over to me to ease me back down.

'Mum, if you don't tell me where he is I will get

up, leave this place and go and find him.' I don't think I could have got up, even if I really wanted to, but I needed answers. I looked deep into her eyes. 'Where is he?'

Mum closed the door, pulled up a chair and just started crying uncontrollably. She cried so much that she started to get out of breath. All I could do was look on until she started to calm down. I was starting to feel properly frightened. Way more frightened than when Mark and his friends had come over to me on the green.

'Please tell me what's happened.'

She took some deep breaths. Held my hand and said 'He's not here, son. Your dad is gone. He went to be with your grandma today. He died.'

I felt as if someone had taken the air out of me. I sank into the bed. The pain in my throat, in my chest disappeared, and I stared at the ceiling, feeling completely numb. Images of the Teddy Boys, of the gang who had attacked me in the park when I was eleven, of Mark and his racist friends flashed through my head. If somebody had done this to Dad, I wanted revenge.

'Who did it?' I asked.

'No one did it, son,' she said. 'He had a heart attack. He was driving the bus. He was heading back to the station. His last trip of the day and he had a heart attack at the wheel.'

I had never heard my dad say that he had a problem with his heart. I looked at Mum, trying to make it make sense. 'A heart attack? A heart attack. He didn't have any heart problem.'

'I know, son. Sometimes it happens. He crashed the bus. An elderly man fell down the stairs on the bus and died too. Leonard, it feel like someone pull me heart from me chest. And look at you. What have we done to deserve this?'

'Nothing, Mum. We've done nothing.' I was feeling numb. I was feeling weak. But I saw the condition she was in and I thought, *I'm going to have to take care of her. I'm going to have to be strong for her.* 'We will get over this,' I said. 'We will get over this.'

I only needed a day in hospital, but I didn't know until I got home that my dad's body was in the same hospital that I was. It was so difficult for Mum. For many nights afterwards, I could hear her crying in her room. We were surrounded by his things; even his work timetable stayed on the table for days after because it was so difficult to throw away anything of his. Even pieces of paper. I used to think that he didn't spend much time with us because of his work, but now breakfast time seemed long, yet incomplete without him. If there was a noise at the door Mum and I would look at each other as if, it might, just might be him. Yet we both knew this was impossible. It was hard to accept that we would never see him again.

Then one day, I was on the high street and I saw a newspaper on a news stand. The headline made me stop and gasp in disbelief.

WAS JAMAICAN BUS DRIVER DRUNK? ENQUIRY BEGINS.

I took the paper down from the holder and as I started to read it, the seller howled at me, 'Hey, you. Are you going to buy that paper or what?'

I was so distraught I put my hand in my pocket and gave him a handful of coins. I didn't look to see how much, but I was sure there was much more money than the paper cost. I walked away and stood on the pavement reading. The newspaper said that there were rumours spreading saying that Dad might have been drinking the day of the accident. I could feel my blood boiling. Dad wasn't perfect, but he was good to people, hard-working, and he never drank, so I knew it was a big lie. It hurt so much because in death he could be getting a bad name, and he wasn't around to defend himself. I threw the newspaper in a rubbish bin on the way home. But when I got home Mum told me that one of her friends had told her about the newspaper stories. They were printed in a few papers, but a couple of days later some other papers defended Dad, and his good name by printing doctor's reports that made it clear there was no alcohol in his blood, and that he died of natural causes.

I'm all she has, she is all I have, and now I have to look after her, I thought, as I watched Mum cook dinner one night, just a few days after my dad's heart attack. I was a teenager, but when my dad died, I really did become a man.

Chapter Twenty-seven

Mum and I spoke about holding Dad's funeral in Jamaica, but Mum insisted that because he'd always said he loved this country so much, he should be buried in England. At first, I didn't feel like England deserved him.

'Listen, Leonard,' Mum said when I tried to argue with her. 'England was where he wanted to make his home, England was where he took his family, an' he had no plans to go back to Jamaica, dead or alive.'

I couldn't argue with that, so we decided to bury him in Southern Cemetery, just south of the city centre. The bus drivers' union made most of the funeral arrangements, so that took a lot of pressure off me and Mum.

On the day of the funeral, I was surprised by how many people turned up. We had no close family in England, but there were lots of people from the now growing Jamaican community who came to pay their respects. There were also lots of local people who had become Dad's friends, and women and men from the bus service who were all dressed smartly in their uniforms. Mr and Mrs Barry came, with Michael and Rosie who both looked so much older. Anna came, though she wasn't my girlfriend any more. We broke up not long after the night of the attack – the night my dad died. We didn't argue; I just had to take care of Mum, but we stayed good friends. She came with some of the other friends that we used to go dancing with. I was so touched by that.

Mum had asked me to make a speech. I had never made a speech in my life. The thought of it made me tremble. But then I thought, *this is not about me, this is about my dad. If I don't do this I might regret it for the rest of my life.* I was nervous, but I had to do something, so I told Mum that I didn't think I could do a speech, but I could recite a poem. Even better I said, I will write a poem of my own. I had never written a poem in my life, but I sat down and wrote a few lines.

In the church, Mum and I sat in the front pew. We had never been in the church before, although we had a meeting with the priest in his lodge, which was on the grounds, but a short walk away from the main building. The church was large. Inside, close to the walls, were tombs of fallen warriors, local nobility and people who made large donations. High up on the walls were stained-glass windows showing Biblical scenes. The seats were made of dark, polished wood, and every word, or cough, echoed around the building. The priest was dressed in a long white and purple robe. He talked for a while about how difficult it can be to lose a loved one, and then he invited me to speak. The church was silent as I walked up to the front of the congregation and stood next to the priest.

'I want to say a few words for my dad, but this is so difficult,' I said, trying to stop my voice from shaking. 'He left us so suddenly, and I still can't believe what happened. Me and my mum are still in shock. I'm not very good at talking but I wanted to say something, so I wrote a short poem.'

I took out a scrap paper from my jacket pocket. I opened it up and began to read.

'My dad loved his family, but he was the special one.
He really was my light of hope, a light that really shone.
He came here from Jamaica, to make a better life,
For me and for my mum, his very loving wife.
I already miss my dad, I really miss his touch.
Me and my loving mum, we miss him very much.
He was loved by many, because he was the best,
And he'll still be loved by many, even when he is at rest.'

I didn't say anything else. I just put the poem back

into my pocket and started to walk back to my seat. The priest patted me on my back as I walked past him. I could see Mum quietly crying, but then the people in the church started clapping. It felt very strange because up until then the church had been very quiet. The bus drivers and conductors stood, and soon everyone was on their feet. The clapping faded as I reached my seat.

'That was so good, son,' Mum said, taking my hand. 'I'm so glad you did it.'

We sang some hymns and then walked to his final place of rest in the cemetery of the church. The priest spoke again, and then some of the bus drivers lowered the coffin into the ground. Now Mum was crying loudly. I put my arm around her, but she couldn't stop. I wanted to cry, but I forced myself not to because I thought it would make Mum cry even more.

We took handfuls of dirt and threw them on to the coffin in the ground, the priest left and went back to the church, and then people stood around talking. But I had to hold on to Mum. When we left the graveside and headed to the car park, a complete stranger, who wore a bus driver's uniform, practically held Mum up with me as she walked. She was weak, so we had to be strong. As I carried her, I realized I was going to have to be strong in other ways, too. I really had to be resilient, for myself and for Mum, for the rest of our lives. I wouldn't have my dad's guidance any more. A thousand thoughts were racing through my mind when the bus driver helping us leaned in close.

'You need to take care of your mum,' he said, as if reading my mind. 'I know you're hurting. I lost my dad when I was young, too. It's tough, young warrior, but you need to step up.'

As we were driving out of the cemetery, I looked back and saw Shirley standing over the grave.

Chapter Twenty-eight

I was no longer an apprentice; I was now Fred's workmate. He had been a painter for his entire life, so it was great to work alongside him. Maybe I wasn't an apprentice any more, but I still needed to get advice from him. Sometimes it was advice about the job, but sometimes it was advice about life. As we were painting one day, I told him about the Maroons, and how important they were to the history of Jamaica.

'Put down your brush,' he said, 'and let me tell you something.' He sat on a closed paint tin, I sat on a step.

'As soon as people started living in communities, other people tried to control them. It has always been a handful of people who are power hungry. But fortunately, there have always been people like the Maroons who have demanded freedom and have been willing to fight for that freedom. We've had, and we still have, freedom fighters here, you know, Leonard. You might look at this country and think we're free and democratic and everything, but once upon a time you couldn't vote if you didn't own land, or if you were a woman.'

He spoke with passion and I listened to every word he said.

'We learn about English history in Jamaica,' I said. 'But Fred, we never learn about the struggles of everyday people.'

'That's it, you see,' he said, leaning over to me as if he was going to tell me a secret. 'Some people think that history is about which queen had a baby with which king, and who that baby went on to conquer. But do you know where history starts?'

'I not sure where it starts,' I said.

'It starts now.' He almost jumped off the tin. 'It starts with me and you. You might not see the importance of it now, but we are making history now. The question is, who's writing it down? Don't leave it to those people who hunger after power, because you'll only get the history of them.'

I thought about what he said, and it made sense. Then he did jump up off his tin.

'Back to work. We need to make history on these walls.'

He wasn't like any of the other older men whom I'd encountered. Everything about him was kind, and his words were wise. He had incredible memories of old England and he just wanted to see builders and painters, teachers and cleaners in the history books. He called me 'one of his own' and by that he meant family. I could sense how proud he was of me when he told people that he had trained me, or when I'd done a good job and he was standing back and admiring the work that I had done.

Together, in south Manchester, we painted a large, empty house. On our last day, we finished early. So after we cleaned away all our tools he threw a clean paint brush to me. He took one himself and started using it like a microphone.

'Come on now,' he said, and to my surprise he started sing the lyrics to 'Wonderful World, Beautiful People', by Jimmy Cliff. So I joined in with him.

We went all the way to the end of the song, then sat on the floor laughing.

'Fred,' I said. 'You know the words to that song better than me.'

'I'm a reggae man,' he replied. 'And there's plenty more where that came from.'

He had the comic timing of Charlie Chaplin and his attempts at Jamaican accents amused me, they weren't mocking, just funny. He genuinely enjoyed the music and appreciated the culture.

172

Mum continued her job as a nurse and was very proud to be working for the National Health Service. I was working even harder. Both of us had to work hard. We had bills to pay and day-to-day living was getting more and more expensive. Every time I saw a red bus pass, my heart ached bitterly. As I got older and started to see that there were many aspects to my personality, I began to think that I only knew Dad as a dad, and that there had been much more to him. I regretted falling out with him when Mum fell out with him, but I understood that people make mistakes. I told Mum how I was feeling.

'Yes, we all make mistakes,' she said. 'The important thing is to learn from them.'

I wanted to learn more about his life, his motivations, his fascinations and obsessions. I wanted to know where he took Mum on dates. I realized that I knew very little about him and it pained me to my core. I knew more about Fred than I did about my own dad. But I was becoming more British and I knew that my dad would be proud of my shifting attitude. He had sacrificed everything to build a better life for me, and here I was, building it myself, without him. He had laid the nest at my feet and it had taken me twenty years to recognize its importance. People were now talking more and more about the Windrush Generation, and

173

I still had the postcard that Dad had sent to me. I wanted to thank him and squeeze him to show him how thankful I was, because I was only just beginning to find out how important that ship was. But it was too late, and I blamed myself for not doing it when I had the chance.

It was my love of music that kept me going, I felt connected to my dad every time his favourite record, 'My Boy Lollipop' by Millie Small, would play on the radio. Sometimes I would sway to the music in three minutes of bliss, before crying like a baby, but I never cried in front of my mum. I stayed stern and I rarely opened up to her for fear of awakening her own grief. Instead, we danced together in frequent celebrations of his life.

Chapter Twenty-nine

There were three things that I cared about more than anything; working, looking after our home, and looking after my mum. Three things, that is, until I fell in love. Her name was Marie Logan. One day I was leaving the house that I was painting, and she was walking past, and she laughed at me.

'What's so funny?' I asked.

'You,' she replied.

'Why?'

'Now let me guess,' she said, rubbing her chin and looking me up and down. 'You are a ... painter.'

'Well, that's obvious. I've got overalls on and they're covered in paint.'

'That's what's so funny. There's paint on your overalls all right, but there's just as much on your shoes, on your hands, on your face, and it looks like there's a whole pot of the stuff in your hair. Were you painting walls or painting yourself?'

I understood what she was saying.

'I had a bad day painting a difficult ceiling,' I said. 'But you should see the ceiling. I did a great job in the end.'

Marie's dad came from a small island called Tobago, which is part of the country called Trinidad and Tobago, and her mum was from a place called Galway, in Ireland. Marie worked as a secretary for a television production company. We met a couple of times in Manchester, and then she asked me if I could decorate her mum's cottage in Cheshire on the outskirts of the city. I promised that I would get most of the paint on the walls. And I did get most of the paint on the walls, but I also got to know her mum really well. She loved baking, so she fed me cakes, and lots of orange squash to drink, as I painted her house. She would stand and watch me eat and work, as she told me what it was like growing up in Galway, Ireland, coming to England as a young girl, and marrying someone from the Caribbean.

Me and Marie would go for night-time strolls and laugh until we ached. Sometimes I would think about my first girlfriend, Anna. I liked Anna a lot, but I realized that my relationship with her was mainly about dancing and having a good time. I felt something much deeper for Marie. She loved nature and I enjoyed describing the countryside around Maroon Town to her. She would listen with a glint in her eyes when I told her about how I would play in the bush, chase and be chased by animals, and eat food that was grown around our house. She was always happy when she saw me happy, and I often thought about how much my dad would have loved her, and how proud he would have been of me. After a year of dating I decided this was the woman I was going to marry – if she wanted to marry me, of course!

Before I left work one afternoon in February, I covered myself in paint – on my hands, neck, face and hair. Just like when we first met. Then I waited outside her office. I was feeling a mixture of nervousness, excitement, and embarrassment. I had to wait longer than I thought, so a lot of people thought I looked very odd, covered in paint and going nowhere. It was tough, until Marie came out.

'Oh, no,' she said as she walked out of the doors and spotted me. 'You've done it again.'

'Yes, I've done it again,' I said. 'But this time I did it to remind you of when we first met.'

I got down on one knee, took out the engagement ring I'd been hiding for two weeks, and said, 'Will you marry me?'

'Of course I will, you work of art,' she said. 'I was waiting for you to ask, and if you didn't ask me by the end of this month, I was going to ask you. It's a leap year, so I'm allowed.'

My mum was delighted when we told her. She hugged Marie so tightly, and I could tell that she was holding her like she was her own.

'This has your dad's hand in it!' she said, tears glittering in her eyes. And I agreed with her.

'Where do you plan to live when you get married?' she asked me, once Marie had gone home.

'I've thought about that, and all is fine,' I replied. 'You can stay here; I will carry on helping you with the rent. I am earning good money and Marie is too. We will find a smaller place to rent so you must not worry yourself.'

'You don't worry,' Mum replied. 'I've decided that I want to retire and return to Jamaica. So, you and Marie can live here.'

Mum had never mentioned anything about returning to Jamaica to me. This left me speechless for a moment. I just wasn't sure I heard correctly.

'What did you say, Mum?'

'I want to go back to Jamaica, son,' she said with her eyes fixed on me.

'Don't go because of me!' I said.

'It's not because of you,' she replied. 'I just want to go back. I feel like Jamaica is calling me again. Your dad and I came here to make a better life for you, and although he's not here, we have succeeded. You will be married soon, and I feel like my work is done. I have to go home.'

My heart sank at the thought of my mum leaving. I now felt a complete sense of belonging in England, and I wanted my mum to witness me flourish like she and my dad had always wanted.

Chapter Thirty

We got married in St Ann's Church on the July 24 1971. I was twenty-three. Marie was twenty-two, and she looked stunningly beautiful. Her beautiful, long, white dress glowed and her eyes were like gemstones as she gazed into mine to take our vows. I could almost feel my dad's presence behind me, patting me on the shoulder and saying, 'There you are, son. You're happy now.' The congregation was made up of some of the friends I has made over the years, but mainly of Marie's family; she had a large Irish family, and they came from near and far to be with us.

Fred was invited of course, and he cried like a baby when I'd asked him to be my best man. I saw him weep again at the wedding, but I didn't bring it up. He kept sniffling during the vows and making weird noises behind my shoulder, but I loved him all the same. Besides, nothing could detract from the beauty of my bride nor the pride in my mum's eyes.

For our honeymoon, we spent a few nights in a hotel on the outskirts on Manchester. Every morning when we woke up, we saw beautiful countryside, and we could go for great walks over hills, down valleys, and along streams. That's what we did every day, and every night we dined in the hotel's luxurious dining room.

On the day my mum was leaving I walked into the living room and found her sitting on a chair surrounded by her suitcases, which I had helped her pack the night before.

'Are you OK, Mum?' I asked

'Yes, son. Me just thinking about everything. Coming here, living here, and now leaving here. Life is strange.'

'I know.'

'You remember when we come here? Two weeks on that big ship. Now me a fly ina plane. I will be in Jamaica later today. What a world.'

I sat on the settee in front of her, then tears rolled down my face. She got up and sat next to me.

'Hey. Things will be fine,' she said putting her arm around me. 'Now the world is getting smaller. You and Marie can come and see me any time. I just feel Jamaica calling me, so me have to go.'

'You don't really have to go.' I said sobbing.

'I feel like I have to go. You will be all right here.

You have a good job, a good house, and you have a fine wife.'

Just then Marie walked in. I could see she had been crying, but she was being organized.

'Sorry. The taxi is waiting outside,' she said.

We jumped up, took the suitcases outside and put them into the car.

The taxi driver must have thought we were crazy. I cried for the entirety of the journey. Marie cried too. Mum was coping better than any of us. She was constantly saying, 'Everything's going to be all right,' in soft tones as we drove. At the airport we got a trolley, put the suitcases on it, checked Mum in, and then walked her to the security gate. Mum had never been to an airport, and I had only been there once with Fred, plane spotting, but Marie knew exactly what to do.

At the security gate, Marie found a moment when Mum was admiring the airport to whisper to me.

'Do you want me to go away?'

I shook my head. 'No way.'

Mum turned to us. 'Well, it's time to go now.'

'Don't forget,' said Marie. 'You want gate eighteen after you pass security. If you need help, just ask.'

'An' you two don't forget,' said Mum. 'Look after yourselves, take care of each other, and come and see me when you have time.'

I just reached out and hugged her. Then I stepped back to let Marie hug her. Then we both hugged her together.

'Take care, Mum,' I said as I held her. 'Contact me as soon as you land.'

'Of course,' she said.

We let go and she walked off. We watched her get her passport checked, then she waved to us, and disappeared into the crowd. Me and Marie leaned against each other, holding each other up, long after Mum had gone. It was some time before we were able to pull ourselves together and walk to the taxi stand.

I saw Marie getting in the back of the taxi, and I decided to ride in the front, but she tugged my arm.

'Come in the back with me,' she said.

I did as I was told. We didn't speak much as we drove, she just took my hand and held it with both hands. There were times when she really squeezed my hand, and I put it all down to the emotions she was feeling after saying goodbye to my mum. I could understand. I was feeling like a part of me had gone too. Marie shook my hand that she was holding, looked at me and smiled gently.

'Can we go for a walk?' she asked.

'A walk. Now. Where?' I replied surprised.

'A park,' she said. 'Let's get some fresh air.'

Knowing her love of nature and the outdoors, I wasn't so surprised now. We had the time, and I thought a walk would do us good.

'Driver,' Marie called. 'Can you please take us to Alexandra Park.'

It was en-route, so we were there in minutes. We said goodbye to the driver and headed for the lake. We walked for a while and talked about how great the lake looked. Then she stopped walking, and so did I.

'From now on, things are not going to be the same,' she said.

'I know,' I replied. 'Now that Mum's gone things will really change.'

'Yes. There's that,' she said. 'And we're going to have a baby.'

'What!' I exclaimed.

'I found out yesterday, but there was so much going on that I thought I would wait until the time was right.'

'Wow,' I said joyfully.

Marie took my hand. 'Leonard, we're going to have a baby.'

Chapter Thirty-one

When baby Grace arrived, I felt my dad's presence so powerfully, that I had to cry even more. I did a lot of crying around this time. Grace was such a wonderful creation. My family was whole. Her skin was the most beautiful shade of brown and her nose was like a sweet little button. I remembered the words of the bus driver at my dad's funeral and I realized I needed to step my duties up to the next level. I finally understood why my dad had such a hunger to make the best life for me. That same hunger got me working six days out of seven; I knew that money was the foundation that would keep us afloat. I dreamt of living in a house, with space, and watching Grace play in the bush like I had done. I wanted the best for her, just as my dad wanted the best for me.

Though I was the happiest I had ever been, there was still something wrong. Not with us, but with the world outside. Sometimes we would still experience racism. One sunny afternoon, when we had taken Grace to the park, Marie was pushing her on one of the swings.

'Hold on tight!' Marie said.

'High-er!' Grace cried with the biggest smile. 'High-er, high-er!'

A white couple walked past, looking towards Grace.

'Aw, look at that little girl,' the woman said. 'She looks like she's about to fly away!'

'She's cute,' said her partner with a shrug. 'But there are enough blacks in the country already, and they don't belong here. They shouldn't be having children.'

I felt myself lucky to have a house and a family, because I knew that there were many black people who didn't have the job opportunity that I had. They didn't have someone like Fred, and they might not have had the start that I had. Some were living in terrible conditions. Breathing in damp and asbestos from rotting houses, unable to find work to better their circumstances. I realized that something was very wrong with the society that we lived in. I saw people on the streets demonstrating for equality, and against racism. I saw black, white and Asian people uniting to fight for a better society, and sometimes I felt guilty, because I was so busy in my world, raising my child and taking care of my family. I just didn't have the time or energy to take to the streets, but I knew something was wrong and really I cared.

In November 2017, we got news from Jamaica saying that mum was very ill. She was ninety years old, losing her sight, losing her hearing, and suffering from high blood pressure. She was also suffering from dementia. Some of my younger, distant relatives were living in the house. This was a new generation. I was getting older, and it was interesting to see how this digital generation used technology. They would call me sometimes to tell me how Mum was getting on, and sometimes they would send me text messages. I was amazed at how I could now just call them from the phone in my pocket. I even saw Mum on a phone app. She recognized me, but could not communicate with me.

The black community in Manchester had changed. It was no longer made up of mainly Caribbean people; there were now people from all parts of Africa, and even places like Fiji and Brazil. The most recent immigrants to the city were people from eastern Europe.

Me and my beautiful wife retired. The house was paid for, but we didn't want to sit back and do nothing. Grace had grown up and was doing well for herself. She went to university and studied Civil Engineering. Her job was overseeing building projects in the North West of England. We were so proud of her.

Grace was earning more money than I ever earned, and she and her friends even went on holidays abroad, but there was something I needed to do. I took Marie back to the lake in Alexandra Park, and back to the very place where she had told me she was pregnant. We were much older, and much slower, but I took her hand.

'I want us to take Grace to Jamaica to see her grandma,' I said. 'I want her to see the house where I was born, and the land that I was raised on. I want her to see where I played as a child and experience just a little of what I had. I wanted her to taste mangos from the trees.'

'That's a great idea,' she replied, gleefully hugging me. 'She really needs to get in touch with her Jamaican heritage. Let's do it.'

So that was it. Before we were too old to travel, we were going to take Grace to Jamaica to see her grandma and Maroon Town. It would be a trip to remember. A trip of a lifetime. That was the plan.

Chapter Thirty-two

That was the plan, but now I'm here. Locked in a cell like a common criminal. I'm seventy-one years old, it's 2018, and here I am, locked up by the country that my parents, and I, helped to build. They told me that it's not a prison cell, they told me it's a detention centre. To get me here they put me in a police cell, and then they brought me to this cell, and both cells look the same to me.

We wanted to take Grace to Jamaica. We just wanted to see my mum. I applied for my passport, but when we arrived at the passport office, the border and immigration officer behind the screen beckoned over two police officers. They threw me against a wall and detained me in front of my screaming wife and daughter. Do you know how bad that feels? It was humiliating. When I shouted out, 'What's wrong? I haven't done anything.' One of the officers shouted in my ear, 'You're not a British citizen, and you have

189

never been a British citizen. You've been living in this country illegally, and so you're under arrest. You don't have to say anything, but it may harm your defence if you do not mention when questioned something that you later rely on in court. Anything you say may be used in evidence.'

'What does that mean?' I shouted.

The other officer whispered in my ear.

'That means you're going back to the bloody country you came from.'

I looked at the man behind the screen.

'What's the problem?' I shouted to him.

'You haven't got a passport, and you're not entitled to a passport,' he replied, emotionless.

My mind went back to the time we were boarding the ship sixty years ago, when I asked my mum why I didn't have a passport. I remembered it like it was yesterday. I told her I wanted a passport, and she told me I didn't need one. I remembered her telling me that her passport is my passport, and that it promised us protection and it gave us the freedom to travel. I was so upset at the time because I didn't have a passport. As the memories came flooding back, I shouted, 'Please check my mum's passport,' convinced that that would stop them.

'Where's your mum?' he asked.

'Jamaica.'

'That's OK then,' he said with a smirk on his face. 'Because that's where you're going.'

I was now getting desperate. An immigration officer came and stood between Marie and Grace, and me. I struggled and protested.

'I travelled on my mum's passport. They told her I didn't need one. The Queen said I didn't need one.'

But they didn't listen to me. I tried to roar like a lion and speak truth, but they just weren't listening.

All my life I did as my grandma said. I tried to do good so that good would follow me. I've worked hard my entire life to make England my home. I have survived being mocked and abused at school. My blood ran down the streets of Manchester when I was beaten. I tried to do the right thing. I've paid my taxes, and I've never broken the law. I thought I was British. My mum, my dad, even Fred, raised me to have pride in this country. Now look at me. Everything is being taken away from me. The prime minister wants to impress her supporters by being tough on illegal immigrants, so she creates what she calls a hostile environment for them, but I'm not one of them. I am not illegal, but because of her I can lose everything.

You'll never believe who I just saw. Remember Winston? The boy on the ship with the strict nanny?

He just turned up here with one of his students. He recognized me straight away. He's a human rights lawyer now. I couldn't believe it myself. He was lucky. He had a passport because he was born in Britain. He went to Grammar School, then went to University, he studied law, and now he's semi-retired, but he still helps people like me. It was great to see him, but I never wanted to see him like this. He said he's going to try his best, but it's going to be difficult. He said the government wants to create the prime minister's hostile environment for people like me, and that's why I'm here. I've never been hostile to the government, so why are they being hostile to me?

Winston and his student have gone away to see if they can make any appeals on my behalf, but he warned me that every week they are deporting people like me, and it doesn't look good. He said I might be on a plane to Jamaica in two days' time, and I might never be allowed back to Britain again. Jamaica's nice, but Manchester is my home. I've lived here for most of my life.

Help me please. I just want to see my mum before she dies.

I love my wife. I love my daughter. I love my country. But now I sit in a cell, caged, desperate, lonely, and alone. I just don't know what's going to happen to me. I want to roar like a lion, but no one can hear me here. I was a dancer. I was a painter. I was a lover. I was a husband. I was a proud man. I was a Windrush child. I think I deserve better.

THIS BOOK IS ENDORSED BY

Human rights are laws that look after all of us. They uphold important values such as truth, fairness and equality. For example, it is a human right to have a nationality, an identity and a home.

Leonard's story is partly about what it means to be British. If you identify as British, it's about how you feel about the UK. But being a British citizen is something that is controlled by the law. Leonard was British by law when he was born in 1947 and also when he was brought to the UK in 1958. But by 2018, the law had changed and the UK no longer saw him as British.

Leonard was one of thousands who came to the UK from the Commonwealth after World War Two. They were all British by law, so they all were free to come and stay in the UK. Many were encouraged to come. They were needed to help rebuild a country shattered by war. They took up jobs in the NHS, the Royal Mail, in public transport, the armed forces and more.

Not everyone was made welcome. Many Black and Asian people suffered discrimination and violence because of their skin colour. That is racism. In the 1960s and 1970s, the government made laws to try and restrict the number of Black and Asian British people coming to the UK. The rights of British people were made unequal, so that some (mainly white) British people remained free to live in the UK and some (mainly Black and Asian) British people were not.

In 1981 Parliament passed the British Nationality Act, a new law that took away the British nationality of thousands of people, including people like Leonard who had made the UK their home. Since 1 January 1983, people connected to the UK under British law are called British citizens. Some are automatically citizens. Others have to apply to register their citizenship.

Leonard did not automatically become a British citizen because, like many thousands of others he didn't know the law had changed or that he needed to do anything about it. The deadline passed. Even people who *did* know didn't necessarily register. The Home Office told many of them there was no need and that it would not make a difference to their rights.

But it did make a difference. It meant they were regarded as guests who needed permission to be in the UK. This permission could be taken away at any time.

Many Black and Asian British people lost their citizenship and were treated as if they had no right to be in the UK. Some were forced to leave the country. The situation became known as the Windrush Scandal. In April 2018, the British Prime Minister and Home Secretary apologized. But the injustice didn't end.

Many people still have to register their citizenship, including thousands of children who have grown up feeling as British as their friends. Some were brought to the UK at a young age and have little or no memory of anywhere else. Many were born in the UK, as were their parents, but haven't been able to register. Children have rights to register as citizens, but the Home Office does not give them the information they need to do so. It also charges over £1,000, which many can't afford.

If you want to stand up for these children and their rights, you could talk to your parents and teachers about discussing the issues at school. You could write to your MP, telling them why citizenship rights should be accessible. Every action you take, no matter how small, makes a difference.

Amnesty International is a movement of millions of ordinary people around the world standing up for humanity and human rights.

www.amnesty.org.uk/education